The Mind Spins

A Collection of Short Stories

The Mind Spins: A Collection of Short Stories
Copyright ©2021 Geza Tatrallyay

ISBN: 978-1-941416-26-6 (trade paper)
ISBN: 978-1-941416-27-3 (ePub)
ISBN: 978-1-941416-28-0 (mobi)

Library of Congress Control Number: 2021913515

Watercolor Abstract Face ©Anna Ismagilova via iStock

P.R.A. Publishing
P.O. Box 211701
Martinez, Georgia 30917 U.S.A.
www.prapublishing.com

the Mind Spins

A Collection of Short Stories

GEZA TATRALLYAY

*For Alexandra, my beloved daughter, who has dedicated
her career as a psychologist to the study of the mind,
its states and its troubles.*

Acknowledgements

I would like to thank my publisher, Lucinda Clark of P.R.A. Publishing, who was kind enough to look at the manuscript and saw the merits of publishing this collection of short stories. Along the way, both she and the editor we worked with, Laine Cunningham, made helpful suggestions to come up with the final product. I am grateful to them and to all the other people Lucinda sought input from, especially Melissa Williams Design for the wonderful cover. I would also like to thank my author friends Christina Starobin, Timothy Niedermann and Keith Steinbaum for reading an early draft and providing the glowing comments on the back cover.

I am also especially thankful to my dear wife, Marcia, who has been a loving supporter of my writing and plays a key role in many of these stories, both in those based on my dreams and in those where a shared life experience was the genesis. My thanks also go to my daughter Alexandra and son Nicholas, and the other family members and friends who became characters in my stories. I hope I have not offended any of them by including them especially in the tales where they are actors in my dreams.

Table of Contents

Part I

AWAKE

These stories were written in a fully conscious state and take place in a world that resembles the reality we live. Several were "spun" out of my indignation at specific examples of social injustice while others were instigated by direct experiences where a somewhat strange element was introduced into my world. I hope the reader shares my concern that these social issues are still so poignantly with us as well as my delight in the more personal stories.

The Purple School Bus

A strange old school bus, painted a bright purple—or was it . . . mauve?—showed up a few years ago on a patch of mown grass among the trees just off the Roland Road. We were shocked when we first saw this brilliantly colored vehicle on one of our trips home, so out of place in the woods of rural Vermont. And we knew it wouldn't be going anywhere, considering the cement blocks in front of the tires and the flowers lovingly planted in a bed that ran along the side.

Indeed, the dilapidated old vehicle was still *in situ* the next time we did our usual loop around the dirt roads just a few days later. It became a regular, if gaudy, fixture—its garish violet hue, stuck in there among the discrete forest colors, jarring the senses—that made us smile each time we passed. The next summer, too, it was still parked on the same patch of grass, the purple perhaps a little less brilliant in its aspect, and the following April, when we came upon it during our first hike of the season, we noticed that rust was starting to appear along its fraying bottom edges.

Was anyone living there? Did someone spend time there when the snows disappeared? Or, at the least, in high summer? It seemed that way, because on several of our walks we noticed a half-empty plastic jug of water or a black garbage bag under the bus, and once, a screened tent was set up behind it. Each season, the flowerbed featured carefully tended pansies and zinnias. But we never saw anyone come or go near the bus, never even glimpsed a sign of human life inside or in its vicinity, ever.

Of course, we wondered about the strange vehicle—who owned it, and how had it appeared on that particular patch of land? Who had painted it bright lavender, and why? And what invisible ghost looked after the dilapidated bus year after year? It even came up during conversations with several of our neighbors, but without fail, they all reported that they had never seen anyone inside or on the adjacent patch of grass. Our friends, too, were intrigued, though: was it an aging hippie who had returned to Vermont after touring the country in his—or her—bus, then decided to park it there and who maybe even now was spending time sitting on a rickety lawn chair out of sight behind it, smoking dope? Might someone actually be living in this ancient transport for school children, and if so, was it fitted out with at least some semblance of habitable living quarters? Or, perhaps had it just been placed there as a quirky piece of work by some artist?

These questions and others—the seemingly impenetrable mystery of the purplish school bus— puzzled us each time we wandered up Roland Road. Marcia or I would inexorably raise such queries when the plum blob appeared in our sights. By the time we returned home, though, our curiosity would have receded: certainly, the enigma of a random amethyst colored school bus parked in the forest somewhere in rural New England was never pressing enough to demand immediate resolution.

* * *

But this one February, I came back to Vermont for a book event. Marcia stayed in San Francisco to look after our two grandsons. And even though the day was misty and freezing, with that bone-penetrating New England cold, and snow and ice made the dirt roads difficult to navigate, perhaps rather foolishly, I decided I needed fresh air and exercise.

So I set out on the shorter version of our usual loop. As I walked up Roland, surrounded by a gray fog that hung in the leafless trees, already from further out the lurid lavender bus stood out against the dusky white snow. The vehicle seemed so out of place, so otherworldly—like an alien spaceship—that I half expected little green Martians to run out and greet me.

All of a sudden, as still from some distance my eyes were roving over the strange vehicle, a faraway unearthly, ghoulish shrieking shattered my reverie and the deathly silence of the winter woods. I stopped dead in my tracks. Could it have been a fox? They screech like that, I tried to reassure myself. Or perhaps an owl?

If not, then what?

I was spooked, but in spite of the eerie atmosphere—or perhaps because of it—when I found myself right alongside where the purple bus was parked, I was taken with this irresistible urge to go up to it and look inside through the frosty and dark windows. Indeed, I wondered, in all the years Marcia and I had passed by this out-of-place rickety vehicle, why had we not checked it out more thoroughly? Why, for heaven's sake, had we always just continued on our walk, blabbing away, without deviating to the left onto the patch of grass to look inside one of the windows?

And why the impulse to do so now? Was it because I was alone? And didn't have Marcia to talk to? Or was it some weird, irresistible supernatural force?

I could feel my heart beat faster as I veered off the road. My boots crunched through the snow, each step bringing me nearer and nearer to the vile violet thing. Once I was close enough to touch the side, I paused to listen, expecting to hear that unearthly scream again. I cast my eyes all around the clearing, but this was mainly to steady my pulse, sure I would not see anyone. It was only then that I raised myself up on tippy-toes and brushed the snow and ice off the window.

Squinting, at first I only saw the rows of torn black leather seats on rusting metal frames. But swiveling my head to the left, at the back, there seemed to be an area where the seats had been taken out and a makeshift table had been added in front of the very rear bench. In the gloom inside, under the table and protruding toward the other side, I perceived what seemed to be a large, organic looking lump.

Desperate now to get a better view, I moved down along the side of the bus toward the back. But the table totally obscured the line of sight through the next window. Frustrated, I trudged through the deep snowdrifts around the rear to the other side, the one hidden from the road, and went up on my tiptoes again to peer through one of the frosty windows there. But in the darkness inside, I could only make out what might have been a blanket or tarp loosely thrown over the shape.

I told myself that it was nothing; probably just an old duffle bag someone had left there, or some garbage. I started to edge my way back through the snow toward the front of the bus and out to the road to resume my walk, wanting to put all this craziness behind me. No, indeed head for home. The air was growing colder, and small, dense snowflakes had started to fall.

I stepped out onto the road again. *That was not just a duffle bag under the table*, I told myself firmly. *Not garbage, either. The tarpaulin had deliberately been draped over whatever needed to be hidden. And the shape . . . it could be a body.*

I could not leave it at that; I needed to know what was under that cover. Reluctantly, I forced myself to turn back to the vehicle and headed, this time for the door.

The cold gripped the door in its frozen jaws. I needed all my strength over a good seven or eight minutes before I was finally able to crack it ajar just a notch, a couple of inches. The door refused to budge any further, despite all my pulling and pushing. I needed some kind of a tool to force it open, I decided. In the descending gloom, I searched for a solid branch to lever it sufficiently so I could clamber inside. I trudged through the snow to a tree at the edge of the clearing, where I found a bough low enough to break off. The snow crept over the tops of my boots and sent trickles of icy water down to my feet.

What am I doing here? This is crazy. I should be at home in front of a crackling fire reading a book or watching the boob tube with a nice glass of cabernet instead of struggling with this stupid purple bus.

But I could not let it go: my subliminal self drove me forward and with almost superhuman force, I broke off the branch, dragged it back to the vehicle, and used it to pry ajar the rusty and frozen door. It creaked open bit by bit until, with a screech almost as inhuman as that of the fox, a gap opened up large enough for me to squeeze through.

Once inside, I shook my whole body and stomped my feet to get rid of the snow that had accumulated on my parka and at the tops of my boots, then inched my way toward the rear of the bus, wriggling my freezing toes. As I approached the table, I began to shiver. Was it the cold, or the creepy foreboding I sensed? I leaned down to examine the blob under the table, and yes, indeed, a dark grey tarpaulin had been thrown over a largish shape. Steeling myself, I pulled back the cover.

My worst fears were realized.

What lay there, in front of me on the filthy floor of the bus, was a ghoulish looking, partially decomposed, half frozen corpse of a partly naked woman, the eyes set deep in the skull staring straight up at the roof of the bus. An immense rusty Bowie knife was stuck in among the ribs under the left breast, with dried blood staining decaying flesh, bones and tattered clothes.

Fortunately, because of the cold, there was no stench, but the horrific sight alone brought me close to retching. I forced myself to look at the remains of this poor human being once more—whoever it was. She was old. Her scraggly white hair clung here and there to the decaying scalp. Her mouth, agape as if gasping for a last breath, held a few rotting teeth. Her wizened figure was contorted into an unnatural pose. In her mid-seventies, I guessed, but could be sixties or even eighties for that matter.

The gruesome remains of some witch, I wryly observed to myself as I threw the tarp back over the corpse to cover it up. Then I quickly cast my eyes around the back of the bus, to see if I could find something that might identify the woman or what had befallen her, but nothing was evident, and, as revulsion, total confusion and the impending darkness dulled my senses, I started to inch my way toward the front. Panic gripped me halfway up the aisle and my only thought now was that I had to get away from what I took to be a murder scene.

As I walked—no, trotted—along the icy road, I constantly

looked back to make sure I wasn't being followed . . . by the murderer or the witch's ghost.

Who was the victim?

Who had murdered her? And why?

Weird at her age, but . . . had she been sexually assaulted? Ugh . . . but possible, looking at her shredded clothes and exposed breasts and midriff.

Or could it have been suicide? Unlikely. Not with that knife stuck into her heart.

How long ago had she been murdered? Maybe last fall, judging from the state of the body, especially with the effects of the cold weather.

Did the victim live in the purple bus, at least part time? Was it she who had tended the flowers and left the signs of life we had noticed over the years?

And then it dawned on me. The murderer could be local—indeed, probably was—and could still be around. Worse, the killer might see my tracks in the snow. Could he or she follow them back to my house? I tried to walk where there had been some traffic, some tire treads on the road, but when I looked back to see if that helped, I saw that for now, my boot prints were still evident in the newly fallen snow. I would have to come back out with my Subaru Forester to obliterate them . . . although maybe by then enough precipitation would fall to cover them over.

Should I report what I found to the police? Of course! But . . . might I become a suspect? I had worn gloves throughout the whole episode in the bus, so I would not have left any fingerprints. And the murder seemed to have taken place some time ago. But still, how would I have known about the site, why had the woman's body remained undiscovered for so long, until I happened upon it? There would be questions . . .

No, I had to report it. The police had to find the murderer. My life was in danger. Plus, it was my civic duty.

* * *

I had worked myself into a state of complete confusion by the time

I got back to the house. Should I call the police first, or should I drive over my boot prints to prevent the murderer from finding me? I finally decided on the latter, largely, I think, because, subliminally, I wanted to see if anybody had shown up. I wanted to know whether someone might be following me.

I grabbed my keys and jumped in the car. As I pulled out of the garage, I saw that the snow was falling in sheets. Any marks on the ground would be quickly covered. My worry was superfluous, I sighed with relief. But, hell, I was already in the SUV and turning out of my driveway, windshield wipers going full tilt and the brights on. Driving was treacherous, but the purple bus wasn't far up Roland Road—which, as a seldom-traveled side street, wouldn't be plowed until the following day sometime. I turned slowly onto the dirt track, with my all-weather tires crunching through the snow.

As I approached the clearing, headlights cut through the curtain of falling snow, spicing up the descending darkness. The vehicle facing in my direction must have been right by the bus. Could it be the murderer's? There was no place to turn around. Besides, better at this point to pretend I was normal traffic. I inched forward, dreading any encounter, but also conscious of the slippery conditions.

There, in front of me, a pickup truck was stopped on the side of the road by the clearing. A long-haired, bundled up man with a goatee stood beside it, calling to a dog gallivanting in the snow. The dog ran between the bus's door and the man, yelping as if there was no tomorrow. The aging hippie—for that's what he seemed to be—waved as if he wanted me to stop. I hesitated a moment, wondering what I should do: if I kept going, that would be unfriendly and appear suspicious. If I stopped to chat, however . . . who knew what that would lead to. My instinct was to keep going but my curiosity and anxious state led me to stop.

I pulled up beside the truck and the longhaired man came over. I rolled down my window and he addressed me. "Hey, man. I need some help."

"Terrible weather. Couldn't be worse." I tried to avoid

answering since I wasn't keen to assist a man who might be a murderer.

"Bro, my pickup slid off the road. You gotta help me!"

No way in hell was I going to get out of the car. I could just see this weirdo knock me over the head with a wrench or stick a Bowie knife or a screwdriver in my side before dragging me into the bus beside his other victim.

"No, I'm sorry. I don't have any chains. Plus, it wouldn't work. My SUV isn't powerful enough for your truck." I was improvising, making the stuff up.

"No worries. I've got a towline. Let me hook it up. You just need to put your foot on the accelerator when I tell you. I am sure your bloody Forester can pull my pickup out of the ditch."

Geez, was he already imagining blood in my cab?

At least that meant I wouldn't have to get out. "I don't know . . ."

"Fuck, man. You're not goin' to leave me here in this godforsaken place in these crazy conditions . . ."

I glanced nervously over at the bus where the dog was yelping away before I uttered a reluctant, "Well . . ."

"Come on, man."

"Okay, but I'm not getting out."

"Sure thing. I'll rig the shit up." He called to his dog. "Hey, Gina, shut yer trap, and come over here and sit."

Or was that meant for the dead woman inside the bus? Was her spirit talking to him? Was she called Gina, too? I was starting to lose it.

The hippie went over to his pickup for the towline. It was then I saw that his vehicle was slanting sideways, with the right wheels ensconced deep in the ditch. But I could also not help noticing that in the back of the truck was a tarpaulin, similar to the one in the bus, covering an organic looking mound.

Oh, God no! He loaded the corpse of the old witch into his bloody pickup and I'm about to help him get it away from the murder site and dispose of it. Before he kills me and dumps my body with hers. Deep in the forest where the coyotes and foxes will devour our flesh. And the ants and maggots will get what's left in the spring.

I shivered, really regretting not having phoned the cops when I got home before coming on this stupid wild goose chase. They would have been here by now, and this murdering hippie would have been arrested. I thought of taking out my cellphone and calling right then, but I knew that would be hopeless since there was no reception along Roland Road. Even if I lucked out, the weirdo would overhear my conversation and do away with me.

He stepped out from behind my SUV.

"Okay, man," he said. "You can start revving it up. All in one go."

I hesitated. I had a choice. I could try as hard as possible to pull his truck out, and we might succeed. In which case, I might be able to get away and get to the police as fast as possible with a description of the man and the truck.

The license plate, yes, I had to memorize the number! But the plate was covered with snow and ice and it was already pretty dark; all I could see in the gloom was that it was green. Vermont.

Or else I could fake it and say sorry, my SUV just isn't powerful enough. But the hippie wouldn't buy that, for sure. He would make me get out of the cab—maybe even at gunpoint, who knows—so he could try, and it would be at that moment that he would knock me on the head with a wrench or kill me some other way. I would be just one more corpse for him to dump.

My best bet was to pull the truck out and as soon as he disconnected the towline from my vehicle, drive away as fast as possible. But what if he didn't detach it and just came up to me and killed me sitting here in my SUV. For that he would need a gun, and so far, I hadn't seen any firearms. He could have a gun in his pickup though . . .

I put my foot on the accelerator and floored it. The engine strained. The pickup moved a little . . . but I just tugged it further up the ditch. The two right wheels embedded even deeper in the snow. The hippie ran up to my window.

"Fuck, man! This is no good. We need a plank or two to put

under these wheels. You don't have a couple by any chance in the back, do you?"

"What do you take me for, some kind of jerk-off carpenter?" I was getting exasperated with this fool's errand and just wanted to get out of there. To save my own skin.

He looked around at a loss. "Well, maybe I can find something useful in that shit-ass bus."

The way he spoke gave me hope. He didn't act like the place belonged to him.

"Isn't that someone's vacation home in the summer? And you're just going to break in there?" I certainly didn't want him to know that I'd also committed the crime of breaking and entering.

"Shit, man, this is an emergency. Why don't you fucking go look for some planks then?"

"I am not getting out of this car in this weather. That's your problem. Besides, I've got to go. My wife is going to wonder where I am." I wanted him to think that someone would come looking for me soon.

"Okay, I'll go see. Just wait and give it one more try. I need to get this truck back on the road."

I had no choice. My vehicle was still connected to his.

The hippie trudged off in the snow toward the bus with Gina at his heels. I touched the door handle, thinking I might jump out, undo the cable, and hightail it away from this godforsaken place. But the hippie spun back around and yelled toward me.

"Shit, man! The steps! The boards will be perfect."

Before I could open my door, he was back with the little makeshift wooden stairs that had led up to the bus's door, ripping them apart to release two flat boards.

"There. These should do." He gave me a sinister smile. "We'll get this sucker out yet."

I saw him disappear under the right side of his truck.

Suddenly, I felt my calf seize and my foot punch down on the accelerator with reckless compulsion, almost as if ordered by an alien force. The engine roared. The SUV lurched forward, tugging the pickup along.

Only a second passed before I heard that unearthly screech again. This time, I knew it was neither a fox nor an owl.

It was when the screaming died down that I finally took my foot off the accelerator.

The truck was out of the ditch. The only sound that broke the silence now was Gina's whimpering. An eternity passed before I opened the Forester's door, stepped out into the snow, and with much trepidation, made my way to the back of the pickup. Behind the rear wheel lay the bloody, flattened body of my hippie friend. Gina was there, yelping and licking her master's wounds.

In an otherworldly trance, I walked around to the rear of the truck, climbed into the back of the truck and lifted the tarpaulin I had seen earlier . . .

Underneath lay three black plastic bags.

* * *

What the fuck was going on?

What was in the bags? Garbage? Really? Some of the hippie's stuff? Or had the bastard chopped up the body of the old hag and stuffed the pieces into these three black sacs to dump somewhere?

The only way to find out was to open them. Or go back inside the purple bus.

I knew immediately, even as my mind came to this conclusion, that I would do neither.

If body parts were in the bags, the hippie was definitely the murderer. And I had acted in self-defense. If not, then—judging from the way he'd referred to the purple bus—he was not the killer, and I just murdered an innocent man.

Did I really need to know? I'd wasted enough of my time and energy on this weird, random circumstance that had crept into my life. What if I just undid the towline, drove back home, and let someone else come upon this horrible scene in the next couple of days after the falling snow had done its thing? Let them find out what was in the bags . . .

Should I go to the police? How would I explain? Breaking into someone's summer home—even if it was a purple school bus—was a crime. How would I prove that I hadn't known the woman, that I hadn't murdered her and returned to the scene of the crime? My story of driving back to the site in a snowstorm to find the hippie and his pickup there, the "unfortunate" accident where he had ended up under the back wheel of the truck—it would all be very fishy.

Now completely calm and at peace, I climbed down from the pickup, undid the towline, rolled it up, and stored it in the back of the dead hippie's truck. With the snow still coming down in sheets, I got behind the wheel of my SUV and drove back to my house, leaving Gina the dog and the two corpses behind for someone to happen upon in the next few days. Or when the snow and ice melted, for all I cared. The police would have to solve the crime—or crimes, if indeed several had been committed—on this deserted rural side road without me.

Back home, I built a fire, poured myself a nice glass of cabernet, lit up a joint, and settled in to watch the movie adaptation of Dostoevsky's *Crime and Punishment*.

Opi and the Sidecar Christmas

"You won't believe this, Geza." Peter's voice chuckled on my answering machine. He must have called from their apartment in Budapest. We had just arrived at our house in wintry Vermont from Vienna to celebrate Christmas with our adult children and other family members. Nicholas, our son, was studying at McGill in Montreal and daughter Alexandra was working in New York— they, and my father and two sisters, brother-in-law and sister-in-law and three nieces were all coming to join us for the holidays.

It was very late, and I was tired, so I almost didn't press the "Play" button till the next morning. Peter's was the first message of note on the recorder.

"You won't believe it." His signature *hyuk-hyuk* snigger sounded like a chicken as he pulled himself together for the killer line. "Opi just called to say his suitcase is all packed. You apparently promised to drive up to Toronto on your motorcycle and take him back in the sidecar to Vermont. For Christmas with you all." Another little snort. "Now, in the middle of winter. That's really nice of you, Gez."

My brother was, no doubt, being sarcastic.

"He's ready and waiting," Peter's message continued. "Oh, yes, do make sure he has a hat and scarf, so he doesn't die of cold on the drive."

Yes, I did believe it—anything was possible with my aging father. His imagination had become more vivid and, I hated to say, somewhat demented with time. But even though I was dead tired after flying across the ocean to Logan, then driving up from

Boston, I could not help laughing as I relayed the news to Marcia. I could just picture yours truly wearing thick, black-rimmed goggles, peering through the falling snowflakes, tooling along on the interstate highway for nine hours on a motorcycle—never mind that I did not have one and had never even driven one—with my wizened father, better known to his loved ones as Opi, crouched low in the sidecar beside me, goggles poised on his half-frozen nose, icicles of snot hanging from one of the nostrils, all bundled up in a heavy overcoat, with a scarf billowing behind him like Snoopy in the Red Baron cartoon . . .

An image that has become vividly etched in my mind, even though it is totally fictional.

* * *

If you knew my father, perhaps you would understand. What he had said to my brother made sense at some level, as the utterings—or mutterings—of older people often do. Certainly, if you deconstructed Opi's call to Peter, most of the elements of his statement were based in reality.

Throughout his entire life, my father loved to laugh, and this was infectious. He delighted in telling a joke and in having others enjoy it along with him. So, I wouldn't entirely put it past Opi—this could have been just a fast one on Peter and me. To make us laugh with him.

That said, there was more in his comment to Peter than just laughter. Much more.

* * *

First of all, the motorcycle with the sidecar.

In his youth, between the wars, my father did own such a vehicle. A BMW R71 with a sidecar, to be exact. And he used to drive it proudly around Budapest and down to Lake Balaton, parading his beautiful young girlfriend, Lily—who, after a whirlwind courtship, became his wife, at age eighteen, marrying the handsome bachelor of twenty-four. Pictures of the lovers show them smiling, standing beside and sitting astride the vehicle with my mother's arms wrapped around his midriff. But I highly doubt that when they went to the several balls during the season, dressed to the hilt in tails and white tie, my mother resplendent in a long gown, it was on the motorcycle and sidecar. Surely my mother's father would have forbidden it!

And who knows, perhaps before he married Lily, my dashing father took other young ladies, too, for a ride in his sidecar, but I would not know about that.

So, at the very least, the motorcycle with the sidecar was real. Just transposed seventy-five or so years in time, four thousand five hundred miles in distance and from pleasant summertime on the hilly roads around Lake Balaton to harsh winter on the Vermont interstate. And I am quite sure my father—who now lived in an old age home in a suburb of Toronto, where we had settled after our arrival as refugees in Canada—had not even seen a motorcycle with a sidecar since those blissful days in Budapest.

But those are just minor details.

* * *

As paterfamilias, there was no question that Opi could, and indeed did not hesitate to ask anyone in his family to do his bidding. Never mind that I might have been exhausted after the arduous trip from Vienna to Vermont, perhaps too tired to jump on a rig, drive five hundred miles in the middle of winter to fetch him, turn around and then speed the same distance back on the icy roads.

Of course, I would do it. Wouldn't any loving son?

Although, by necessity, as I was growing up, I had learned always to listen carefully to the advice and requests that came my way from my parents, to take whatever was said on board, but still, in the end, to do whatever I felt was right.

Fortunately, Opi and Omi had come to trust my judgment, certainly by the time I was fully grown.

I could have simply refused to fetch my father in the sidecar, no hard feelings. Indeed, since I did not have access to a motorcycle with a rig, I would have had the perfect excuse.

* * *

It, too, was not out of the question that my father may have just finished what he thought was packing his bags when he called Peter. That activity was second nature to him. Throughout his life—especially after my mother passed away—he had always been on the move, traveling the world with his suitcase to seek out friends and family in the most remote places. And the more exotic the destination, the better.

In fact, when I was transferred to London, the very next day after our little family settled into our temporary accommodation in Kensington—which my then employer, the Royal Bank of Canada, paid for while we found something more permanent —my father was there on our doorstep, carry-on suitcase in hand. The children, who were delighted to see their grandfather, ended up having to share a bedroom so we could accommodate our rather inconvenient first guest. But he was Opi, the paterfamilias.

Through one of Peter's friends who owned a travel agency, my father even managed to register himself as a travel agent so he could get all sorts of freebies and discounts on voyages. This was vintage Opi. Above all, he relished getting deals on everything. Perhaps this reflected his immigrant background, the fact that he and Omi had started over as refugees in Canada with nothing. To his dying days, he kept this trait.

Cruises were his favorite sort of voyage. With his travel agent card, he managed to get substantial discounts on some lines, supposedly to check them and the particular itinerary out for the travel agency's customers. So, one day when Marcia came upon an article in a travel journal that mentioned free cruises for mature single gentlemen, provided that in return they would be ready to dance with the many spinsters on the boat, she immediately thought of Opi. She enthusiastically brought this to his attention, thinking that he would jump at the opportunity, and . . . she was completely floored by his rather offended response: "But, my dear, I am not a gigolo!"

Several times when we visited Opi in the old age home where

he spent his last years, we would arrive to his room only to find a partially packed suitcase open beside his bed, occasionally with half-devoured salami sandwiches, opened containers of yogurt and moldy jars of *Noszlopi*, his favorite Hungarian hot sauce which Peter's wife, Sue, regularly supplied him with, mixed in with his pajamas and unpaired socks and underwear.

Oh, the caprices of getting old!

* * *

And ah, yes, Yuletide! By far, Opi's favorite time of year. He would never miss a family Christmas, even if it meant traveling a great distance in an open sidecar in the middle of winter.

That said, our family Christmases were indeed very special. We celebrated, and still celebrate them, the way Opi and his beloved Lily, my mother, used to. With, of course, a few adaptations. (Marcia and I claim these are improvements.)

Even now, it is Christmas Eve that is special for us, just as it is for most Europeans. As it was when the family event used to be at Opi's and Omi's in Don Mills, the Toronto suburb where they had their bungalow. To this day, when Marcia and I are the hosts—as we were that fateful Christmas when I was supposed to fetch Opi in the sidecar—everyone dresses up for the occasion, all the wrapped presents are arranged under the tree, the conifer carefully chosen and set up a few days earlier is bedecked with beautiful hand-carved and blown glass ornaments, the white electric lights replacing the fire-hazard candles of old are lit, and everyone waits expectantly in another room, while the mythical spirit of Christmas (whether the baby Jesus or Santa Claus or Amazon.com has become blurred in our transcultural version) comes to visit to give his, her or its *imprimatur* . . .

And then, the ding-a-ling of some bells—now, rung by me, in days gone by, by my father—indicates that it is time for all to enter the living room. The baby Jesus has blessed the event, Santa has gone back up the chimney, and the Amazon drone has delivered all the presents.

Children first, in order of ascending age; their parents

next—one of the nieces pushing Opi in the wheelchair—and then the older ones, that is, my generation, for whom the magic of Christmas has changed from the opulence of the gifts and the lights and the decorations to the wonder and warmth of being with loved ones. The lit-up and decorated Christmas tree spreads its warm glow throughout the room, as in the background, carols play, and in the fireplace, crackling flames add to the ambience.

The spell is then broken by someone saying in either a close-to-tears (Opi or one of my sisters) or a somewhat sarcastic (most likely, my son, Nicholas or yours truly) voice, "Lovely!" as I struggle to find the track for "Silent Night"—or these days, click the Spotify icon on my iPhone—and we delight in singing along, some of us off-key, the more mature ones in the group tearing up with thoughts of loved ones not present, the younger ones eagerly casing out the mountains of colorfully wrapped presents all ready to be opened, piled under the tree.

Mutual hugging and kissing and the wishing of *Merry Christmas!* follow the dying away of the last strains of the carols—for "Silent Night" is always followed by "Oh, Christmas tree." Then, as my brother-in-law Don assumes contorted poses with his enormous camera and rather phallic lens to snap myriads of pictures, I pop open a couple of bottles of Veuve Clicquot, Marcia and my sister Clara bring in platters of shucked Malpeque oysters, garlic shrimp on sticks, and little toasts spread with chunks of *foie gras mi-cuit*.

While those of us approaching or exceeding the drinking age clink glasses, those palpably younger attack the piles of presents until one of the oldies brings order to the gift giving and opening. It is formally declared that the youngest will start with a present for him or her from under the tree, and then he or she will choose one randomly from the pile and hand it to its intended recipient, aided of course by the order demanding oldie (usually Marcia or my sister Clara).

And so on, until amidst delighted *oohs* and *ahhs* and the occasional *thank you* and kiss of gratitude, all the presents have been distributed to their rightful owners and I have more or less managed to collect the torn wrapping paper and packaging in a garbage bag, or used some of it to stoke the fire, vainly trying to save any somewhat intact pieces and lengths of colorful ribbon for future Yuletides.

After several declarations that this has been the "best Christmas ever", the ladies in the group repair *en masse* to the kitchen to bring to the beautifully set dining table the delicacies prepared earlier for the Christmas Eve meal. I fetch the wine, a St. Émilion Grand Cru opened earlier for the red, an Entre Deux Mers straight from the fridge for white—while Opi and my sister Susan surreptitiously stuff the remaining *hors d'oeuvres* into their mouths and Alexandra and Nicholas and the cousins race to down the unfinished contents of dangerously poised champagne *flûtes*.

After I point out my reserved seat at one corner, everyone finds their place and the noise of scraping chairs is punctuated by the now repetitive and somewhat boring *oohs* and *aahs*. In the middle of the linen tablecloth, in pride of place, sits a cold poached salmon procured the day before and prepared in the morning with much love by Marcia, skin carefully peeled off, and meticulously decorated with slivers of red peppers, olives and dill greens, to be consumed with a cold cucumber sauce. Alongside the fish platter, on separate serving dishes, are thin slices of prosciutto San Daniele and Csabai, a spicy Hungarian sausage, as well as an array of Vermont cheeses augmented with Société Roquefort and Comté from France, a quinoa salad speckled with pomegranate pips, seedy and multigrain iterations of my homemade bread and various condiments. Everyone digs in; no one, not even my niece who is usually a rather selective eater, holds back. Opi proves that he still has a healthy appetite, at least for the delicious home-cooked Christmas meal Marcia has masterminded. Much wine is consumed—indeed I have to go back down to the cellar for a third bottle of the St. Émilion.

But the *pièce de résistance* comes at the end. For dessert is an Austro-Hungarian specialty that has been refined over the many centuries of Habsburg rule, yet each iteration is unique. Mine is a version of my mother's. She, it must be said, could have been a master chef, certainly for pastries, not just at Gundel's in Budapest, but any Michelin-starred restaurant. The delicacy is known as *beigli* in Hungarian and for Opi, as it is now for all of us, no Christmas is complete without it. And the "it" needs to be home baked.

De rigeur, there must be two kinds of *beigli*: one filled with a ground poppy seed stuffing, the other made with freshly ground walnuts. But it is not as simple as that. The poppy seed for the filling has to be finely ground to release the rich, flavorful oils. The paste is then usually combined with melted butter and varying amounts of sugar—I replace the sugar with Vermont maple syrup (actually, also in my walnut filling)—raisins soaked overnight in rum, zested organic lemon and a touch of apricot jam or grated apple. The walnut one is similarly doctored with like additives. The concoction is rolled in a pastry made with lots of butter and eggs and baked until golden brown. The key to the art of *beigli* baking is that the pastry should be as invisible as possible, yet still hold the rolls together. Best served with a Tokaji Aszu 6 Puttonyos or Tokay Esszencia, my father always said. In a pinch, Chateau d'Yqem or even a Trockenbeerenauslese will do.

After dinner, while the hosting team cleans up with the help of those who can still move and are so inclined, the members of the younger set inspect their gifts and show them off to Opi and to each other. Then some games—these days, it's usually Celebrity, introduced to the family by Alexandra during her college days—accompanied by a selection of brandies, *pálinkas*, slivovitzes and other *eau de vies*, and perhaps tangerines and chocolates for those who favor a healthier postprandial treat.

As the fire turns to embers and the energy of even the youngest starts to ebb away, some members of the group say good night and peel off with kisses all around. Opi, too, decides that he should finally turn in on this loveliest of Christmas Eves.

* * *

The next day, of course, we always do the Christmas morning thing with stockings on the mantelpiece for the wee ones (I sometimes attach a dirty sock alongside for fun, hoping against all hope that the more secular Santa or at least Amazon, if not the baby Jesus, will indulge me . . .), so we do combine the European with the North American way of celebrating yuletide. And for the main midafternoon meal, Marcia prepares a delicious turkey with foie gras and chestnut stuffing that is to die for, and the *beigli* is served up again for dessert. Indeed, it remains the dessert of choice for at least ten days after the celebrations, until all the pastry is consumed, and the last crumbs are deemed too dry for human consumption.

* * *

It was for such a family Christmas that Opi wanted me to fetch him in the sidecar. As it was, we did not have to resort to such desperate measures. He flew to a nearby airport with my sister Susan, who also lives in Toronto, and met up with my other sister Clara and her husband Don, who arrived at a similar hour from Chicago.

The sidecar Christmas was one of our last times with Opi, and one that we will all cherish fondly. As we treasure all our memories of this wonderful man, who so deeply loved and marked each and every one of us.

The Abandoned Bra

Marcia found an abandoned bra the other day. Forsaken in the bottom drawer of the rickety green wooden chest in Alexandra's room, which serves as the main guest quarters in our Vermont vacation house. We had come back in April for a couple of weeks, and she was looking everywhere for something our daughter thought she had left behind at Christmas.

A DDD-cup. Definitely not our Alexandra's. Nor could it be Fanni's, our daughter-in-law's, who is rather petite. Moreover, it could not belong to any of my nieces, who are similar in build to Alexandra, tall and slender, well-proportioned. Besides, this undergarment was fairly simple—not the kind any of these sophisticated young ladies would wear.

So, then whose might it be, this mystery bra? Certainly not Marcia's—her breasts are just right to give her the curves I love. Nor mine, I assured her: after all, I am not a cross-dresser. One of my two sisters', perhaps, since they are more robust in the chest than the rest of the family? Not possible. They hadn't visited for several Christmases, and we would have no doubt heard from them if they had left behind such an integral article of clothing.

She and I racked our brains as to which of our recent female visitors might have been so well-endowed, but no one came to mind. We asked Alexandra and Fanni whether they had any idea as to the provenance of the enigmatic item of lingerie, but no. Fanni even requested a picture to send to her mother in Budapest as she had stayed with us sometime before Christmas. The answer came back, "Definitely not!"

We had hosted very few other overnight visitors during that

period, and to our recollection, none of our female guests sported large enough mammary glands to fill a DDD-cup bra. So, how did this perplexing piece of underwear enter our abode and end up in the bottom drawer of an otherwise empty chest?

* * *

I lost several sleepless nights over this hanging question. I urged Marcia to enquire with the woman who cleaned our house every several weeks or so—she was one of the few people who had a key and an alarm code—whether she had any idea who might have left the item of lingerie behind. I even tried to make a joke out of it: the cleaning lady no doubt would confess that the bra was hers, and that she had been engaging in secret trysts at our place. Marcia vehemently dismissed the idea as totally stupid and verging on obnoxious. When it came right down to it, I had to agree that she was probably right since Madge was a proper and good soul. Nevertheless, it was clear to me that to solve this mystery, we would have to think outside the nine dots.

The notion of a secret tryst, though, held some attraction . . . apart from the obvious titillation factor. It gnawed at me. And it did not take a lot during those nights for my obsessive self to be convinced that I was on the right path. For how else could an unknown woman, or perhaps someone of transgender persuasion, leave behind an undergarment? Someone—indeed most likely a couple—must have entered our house unbeknown to us and, at the very least, undressed, leaving behind the bra. She—they—could have taken a shower, slept in or on the bed, and if it were two or more, made passionate love. There were no limits to what my imagination conjured up in the dark. And heaven forbid . . . maybe their coupling had been on our king-size bed!

Or another possibility: since Marcia found the offending item in a drawer, perhaps they had unpacked a suitcase and simply overlooked the bra when they were packing up. Either way, I became indignant when the thought that someone had stayed at our house without our permission percolated in my frenzied mind. I would not rest until I got to the bottom of this enigma.

The next morning, while Marcia was in the shower, I went into the guest room to check the bed and the sheets. No signs, no strange spots or stains, nor indeed faint lingering smells pointed to an unknown presence, or for that matter, any compromising activity. I had already scanned our bedsheet for stains as we were making it in the morning and neither of us had remarked on any persistent untoward odors.

Over breakfast, I broached the subject again with Marcia. After much discussion, I convinced her that, at the very least, she should ask Madge whether it had been she who had placed the bra in the drawer and if so, where she had found the abandoned DDD-cup.

* * *

I was sitting on a kitchen stool reading my email when Marcia posed the question. At first, Madge was visibly taken aback. Then I could see on her face that she was racking her brain . . . and a switch to a frown indicated that her memory had clicked in.

"Yes, you're right. I did find a . . . bra some time ago." She paused, blushing as she continued. "In the guest room . . . your daughter's. Beside the chest of drawers. On the floor. I folded it up and put it in the bottom drawer." And then she added, "I'm sorry. I meant to tell you when you came back . . ."

"Do you remember when that was, Madge?" Marcia asked. "More or less . . ."

Madge took a moment to reflect before answering. "Oh, it must have been three or four months ago. Yes, when I came to check the house. After you left at Christmas. Must have been late January, because it wasn't the first time I came by then."

Listening while still looking at my laptop, I felt my heart speed up. "But you checked all the rooms the times before too and didn't see anything, did you?" I asked nonchalantly.

"Yes. I could've missed it. It was down on the floor. On the far side of the chest from the door."

"Did you notice anything else strange in the house that one time? Anything at all, Madge?" I had taken over the interrogation.

After all, we were not only paying her to clean but also to stop by once a week to make sure everything was all right when the house was vacant.

She was a little taken aback by the aggressiveness of my questioning, but eventually answered with a firm, "No, nothing."

"Thank you, Madge," I said, letting her off the hook.

While I was quite disappointed that she didn't confess to leaving a bra behind after a secret noontime encounter with a lover, at least her answers were shaping the certainty in my mind that someone else might have done so, toward the end of January. Or, at the very least, that a woman had been in the house without our invitation or permission and had left the undergarment in question behind.

* * *

But how would that individual or individuals have entered? They would have needed a key and the alarm code. Beside Madge and ourselves, only Jim, a really good local friend, had both. There was one other key "out there" and that was hidden in a secret place outside. We had only told our children about this hiding place, admonishing them never to tell anyone. More than likely, with their busy lives, they'd forgotten about it.

So how then could somebody gain access to both the key and the code? And more importantly, who?

Several sleepless nights passed as I ruminated on this perplexing question before a possible solution emerged. As an aside, I firmly believe that one often resolves seemingly unsolvable issues in the dark in a half-awake, half-dreaming state. And this is exactly what appeared to happen with this difficult case.

* * *

The guy from the security company who regularly came to service our alarm! The idea flashed like lightning through my brain and pushed everything else out.

Yes, he would have the code—or a code—to get in, that was for sure.

And the key—well, he must have been lucky and found the one outside. Or . . . or perhaps he had taken one of the several spare keys we kept for our guests in a kitchen drawer one time when we had left him there on his own.

With a smug smile, I jumped out of bed and sneaked downstairs, trying not to wake Marcia, and turned a light on only in the kitchen. In the drawer, I found two keys to the house. I cursed aloud—I couldn't remember—had there been three or two?

Marcia might know. I turned off the light and climbed up the stairs and into bed, eagerly awaiting first light so that I could ask my wife this all-important question. The fretting though, started again. So, what if this alarm guy took one of the keys and with the code he was given by his company to service our alarm, entered the house? It still did not explain how the undergarment ended up in Alexandra's room. Surely this security agent was not the one who wore the bra!

A lively mind finds a solution to everything. I remembered that on one of his service visits, the oversized alarm guy, Dave—his name finally came to me—had an equally large woman with him in the cab of his pickup. And yes, relying on my memory and an expert eye for sizing such things up, the DDD-cup would have been right for that lady. Dave must have brought his paramour along in January, and they'd come into the house to pursue a secret love affair. She and he were probably both married with kids and wanted to keep their illicit encounters from their spouses. Hence, our friend had devised this clever way to have their trysts in a place that was neutral territory. And, if someone ever happened to catch them, he could always say he was performing the mandatory testing on our alarm and had his woman along just to keep him company—not something that would raise eyebrows in rural Vermont.

The very next morning, over breakfast, I tried my theory on Marcia. She said, "Not again!" when I first broached the subject, basically telling me that I was severely trying her patience with my obsession with the backstory of the bra. And when I laid out my thinking concerning the man from the alarm company, she said, "Geza, I am really starting to worry about you. You seem to have gone off the deep end. Perhaps you should go see someone for help."

I was so flustered that I didn't pursue the question of the keys. I was no further ahead, and, in fact, half a step back as Marcia had prompted me to question my own sanity . . .

Nor did I receive encouragement when I checked whether the key we had hidden outside was still in place. It was there, but in the end, I decided, so what? Dave could have put it back after using it to get in, just as we always did.

It seemed that Marcia was happy to brush the whole found lingerie episode off as one of those questions such as "Is there a God?" or "How did the universe begin?" for which there is no real answer, or else, that the resolution is so simple that we just had not come upon it. Neither of those easy ways out would satisfy my curious mind.

* * *

But how to get proof that my latest crazy idea was the solution to the conundrum of the DDD-cup?

I was determined to go about this systematically, just like Sherlock Holmes or Miss Marple might have done. First, I needed to know whether indeed Dave had officially come to test the alarm in the timeframe Madge had identified. Marcia usually scheduled these visits for when we were at the Vermont house, but who knows, maybe this time she hadn't. She pretty much always checked with me regarding the timing of any appointment, and I certainly had no recall of discussions around an alarm diagnostic visit.

I could also check her calendar where she religiously recorded any engagement of this nature. The little date book was usually on her desk, so I managed to peek in there surreptitiously while Marcia was cooking dinner. There was no date and time scheduled for Dave or anyone from the alarm company to come to our place since we'd left the previous summer.

Just to be sure, the next time my wife went out on an errand,

I called the security firm to ask whether they had sent someone out in January. The answer was a definitive no.

So that was it then: if Dave had come to our place with his lover, he must have done so on his own, without official prompting or rationale. Which made the infraction even more outrageous.

* * *

How then to take this quest further?

It seemed that any semblance of gaining clarity on how Dave—and by this time, I was pretty stuck on my theory that it was he and his woman who had "used" our house—or indeed anyone else, had invaded our place and left the offending bra behind had dissipated. The only path to the truth, I concluded, would be to try and catch the culprit in the future, if he would deign to return because he had enjoyed himself so much on our guest queen—or worse still, our very own well-used king—that he would want to repeat the experience. And the best way to do that, I told myself, would be to mount hidden cameras to film the couple *in flagrante delicto.*

After a week or so of not talking about the subject, I mentioned to Marcia that I'd been thinking of installing cameras as an added safety measure. She was extremely security conscious, so I was confident that it would not take a lot of persuasion to convince her. Indeed, I was glad not to have to embarrass myself by bringing up my latest theory about the origins of the bra, although she might have suspected something like that was behind the cameras.

"You know, there is more crime around here now," I said, "and it would be a good idea to catch any burglars in the act."

I did not tell her I had already ordered the Google Nest cameras, nor that in fact they would arrive the very next day. It took me just a couple of hours to install one at the front door, one in the kitchen, and one in each of the bedrooms. Perhaps overkill, but I wasn't taking any chances. The timing couldn't have been better, because we were scheduled to go back to San Francisco a few days later, at the beginning of May, and I wanted them in place before we left.

* * *

I was not at all sure that Dave and his paramour would visit during the short month we would be away, but a couple of weeks later, I was thrilled when my iPhone beeped to notify me that the cameras were picking up someone entering the house. I quickly switched to live view.

"Yes!" I hooted victoriously. The camera scanning the front door showed what I recognized to be Dave's pickup drive up and come to a screeching halt. The big man and his equally chunky woman got out and lumbered up the stairs. Dave pulled out a key, opened the door, and disabled the alarm. Just like that, these uninvited guests were inside our home!

The picture switched to the kitchen camera which showed Dave closing the door and dropping his backpack. The two lovers wasted no time to embrace and started pawing each other. Amidst their moans, I deciphered the name *Janie*—and it was she who disentangled first, wiped her mouth, and rasped lustily, "Come on, Dave. Let's go upstairs." Her man picked up his backpack and disappeared off the camera, tugging Janie along.

A few seconds later, to my great consternation, the camera installed in our bedroom showed the two enter. Dave opened his backpack and whipped out a crumpled sheet which they hurriedly spread over our bedspread. I felt affronted by their invasion of our private love nest, but I must say, I was glad they had brought their own bedding.

Without much further ado, they were back at it, literally tearing each other's clothes off and wildly French kissing. Once their rather blubbery bodies were fully naked, Dave hoisted Janie onto the bed, and they proceeded to make passionate love. I will leave out the details, since they are not really relevant to the story. Suffice it to say, it was quite a sight.

Oh, before I forget: this time, too, the bra ended up in the corner. As far as I could determine from the video, it was the same brand and color as the DDD-cup in our possession. But once the lovers had satisfied their hunger, this piece of lingerie too went back on the oversized feminine body along with all her other clothes.

* * *

So now I thought I had the answer to the question that had given me sleepless nights for months. And I had evidence in hand identifying the culprits. What to do with the information and the proof, though?

Well, I could have turned it over to the police and brought charges against Dave and his paramour. However, it didn't seem right to put a man behind bars for wanting to find a time and a place to pursue his love for a woman, even though it meant committing what was after all a crime in anybody's books: breaking and entering. They hadn't taken or damaged anything, and in fact, had used their own sheet, and had straightened up the duvet and pillows afterwards. No, this was not a crime in my books. Just . . . well . . . maybe a peccadillo.

Alternatively, I could have downloaded the videos and sent them to Dave's employer with a letter of complaint about their service agent who was abusing his duty in such a flagrant way. This, too, didn't feel right. At the minimum, Dave would have lost his job and never received a favorable reference from the company. It would have destroyed his livelihood, maybe also Janie's if she was a coworker or if the company were to go after her as his co-conspirator. And it would really have been their children who would have suffered. It could have ended in divorce for both of them, and Dave would certainly not have had the wherewithal to pay alimony or child support. No, this did not appeal to me either.

And then I hit upon it. The perfect solution. I would send the videos and the extra bra to Dave. I would write him a letter telling the story of how I ended up filming them *in flagrante delicto* and why I chose not to go to the police or his company. But that if I ever caught him again or heard from others of similar infractions, I would do exactly that.

I would also get an estimate for changing all the locks on the house—which was probably overdue anyway—and ask him to send me a check to cover the cost as a sign of his penitence and to ensure that he could not use the hijacked key or a copy. After all, there had to be some cost for his offending bravado.

It took a bit of work to get Dave's address, but these days everything is possible using social media, town records, and other sources. It was with great elation, once back in Vermont, that I wrapped the bra and a USB stick with the downloaded videos into a package with my letter and took it to the post office. I vaguely thought I should have asked him to cover the postage as well, but I decided I would write the $3.15 off as the price for the pleasure of having played detective.

Within ten days, an envelope appeared in our Post Office box with Mr. Dave R's return address. I eagerly tore it open and pulled out a piece of notepaper wrapped around a check for $600. On the note was written *Thank you*, signed Dave and Janie.

I never saw Dave again.

The Teddy Bears

There it was, in front of her finally: the four meter high wall built from concrete blocks, the many coats of paint chipping off in places, the barbed wire on top rusting with age. And the equally dilapidated walkway that ran alongside, broken here and there, with dandelions flowering in the earthen cracks. There were the occasional strips of dead grass dotting the dry dirt that separated the sidewalk from the busy road in front, and the regularly spaced telephone poles displaying wind-torn, garish notices stuck there by wanton immigrant women offering their services. Anna smiled when low in a nook in the wall, she saw the familiar makeshift altar bedecked with the burnt-out, mostly melted candles, withered flowers and—one in each corner—the teddy bears they had left behind. In the middle, on the wall, scored in red letters on a gold oval background, the word that made her heart leap: *Rejoice!*

Nevertheless, it was with sadness and trepidation that Anna looked at the little shrine she'd helped her father and mother erect out of the stones and bits of concrete broken off from the barrier. They'd built it shortly after their arrival to celebrate their successful border crossing after the perilous journey across Mexico, all the way from Guatemala. She smiled as she remembered placing her two teddy bears—Godfredo, the furry little animal she'd trucked all the way from home, and Esperanza, the one given to her by her cousin—in the rear corners of the altar. As on each visit, she blew them a kiss, and repeated her wish that they would bring her mother and father back to her.

Anna remembered how her mother, Isabella, had announced,

"This is it! Let's give thanks for our fortune here," when she had seen the red letters on the gold background. Those happier times, just a few days ago, when the family was still together and, although they'd arrived with nothing, they had the future to look forward to. That had certainly been something to celebrate, especially when they looked back on the life they had left behind.

Carlos De Leon had been forced to leave his homeland after the Mara Salvatrucha gang made it clear that he and his family were targets. The gang had continually increased the dollar amounts they extorted to allow him to pursue his thriving little export business and when, finally, he said he could no longer pay, they threatened to take his daughter and wife in lieu of cash. He knew what that meant, for it had happened to the daughter of one of his friends. Isabella and his darling little Anna would be forced into prostitution, or worse still, sold as sex slaves.

Carlos had no choice. They had to leave.

Where could he go with his small family? The United States was where his brother had emigrated to years earlier, so that was where he would try his luck. Secretly, he'd always wanted to follow in the elder De Leon's footsteps. In fact, Isabella and he had given their daughter a name that was as familiar in America as in Latino culture with that in mind. But getting there meant risking two border crossings and a dangerous trip across Mexico. And the reception in the US seemed, from the word-of-mouth reports filtering back, not necessarily positive. In fact, the most recent news was that prospective refugees were being turned back at the border. Only a very small number, if any, were processed each day and allowed to enter. Never mind, Carlos decided, even if they had to cross illegally, better to take their chances than await certain death for himself and a fate worse than that for his beautiful wife and young daughter.

The family left Guatemala City. Carlos closed up his business and dug up the little money he'd buried under a bush while Isabella packed a change of clothes for each of them. They said goodbye to their small house with mixed feelings and took several buses to get to the Mexican border, telling Anna they were going to visit her cousins, Jorge and Victoria, in California. The only toy she was allowed to take was her beloved teddy bear, Godfredo.

They stayed away from *la bestia*, or *el tren de muerte* as it was also known, traveling rather by bus or on foot between cities, finally reaching the US border at Mexicali. Here, Carlos contacted Juan, a coyote and a friend of his brother Felipe. Juan confirmed that very few migrants were getting through legally at the border crossings, and the only way, really, now would be over the wall, across the river, or through the desert. Juan knew the best place and time to cross the old fence—not the portion of Donald Trump's barrier that had been completed.

A little after midnight several days later, Juan took them to a point along the border. He propped a portable ladder up on the Mexican side of the fence, climbed to the top, and slid a second ladder down on the American side for the little family to make their escape. They quickly merged into the night and made their way to the house of another friend of Felipe's in Calexico.

The next morning, this man drove them to East Los Angeles where Felipe lived with his wife Selena and their two children. Carlos and Isabella were finally reunited with their relatives and spent much of the day catching up on all the news, especially the latest political developments that could affect the newly arrived refugee family. Felipe told them that the President had made it next to impossible for illegal entrants to obtain asylum and, in fact, Immigration and Customs Enforcement, or ICE, agents were known to stop Latinos on the streets or make unannounced house calls in search of migrants without papers. They would have to be careful and hope for the best; perhaps a future change of government would ease the rules again.

Anna was oblivious to this bad news and was delighted to get to know her slightly older cousins. She was overcome with emotion when Victoria gave her Esperanza, the little teddy she'd grown up with, so that Godfredo would not be alone. Isabella allowed her daughter to stay up extra late playing with her new-found cousins and the teddy bears and when, finally, she decided to put her to bed, she told her that the next day they would explore their new country.

After a well-deserved rest and a hearty American breakfast, Carlos, Isabella and Anna went out for a long walk to tour the neighborhood and buy a few things with money Felipe lent his brother. Their spirits were high—the weather was beautiful, they were in their new homeland, free of the threats to their lives, and ready to embark on a new and rosy future . . . although getting legal residency papers did seem difficult. But never mind that for now, they were in the USA!

On their way back home, after turning a corner, they came upon the multicolored, decaying concrete wall. Seeing the bright red graffiti, *Rejoice!* set in the gold rectangle, Isabella, on a whim, decided they should erect a little shrine in gratitude for their good fortune. And to preserve the memory of the many fellow *Guatemaltecos* and other Latinos who did not make it. Once the makeshift altar was built, Isabella and Carlos were touched when Anna told them that she wanted to leave her teddies there. She was a grownup now and didn't need them anymore, she said, as she placed one in each corner.

Isabella added a couple of the candles from the dozen Selena had asked them to get for the dining room table, and Carlos separated out a couple of the flowers from the bouquet they were bringing her. Finally, Anna begged her parents to leave some of the bread and fruit they had bought in case the teddies got hungry. When the little altar was well stocked, Carlos suggested they say a few prayers. They bowed their heads in silence, and Anna saw that her mother had tears in her eyes.

Just as they finished giving thanks, Carlos saw two ICE agents approach out of the corner of one eye, and remembering what Felipe had told him, he whispered to Isabella to run while he grabbed Anna in his arms and took off in another direction to split up their pursuers. The agents hesitated a moment to discuss tactics and then one came after him while the other, a female, took off in pursuit of Isabella.

As the burly male operative came closer and closer and went

to pull out his sidearm, Carlos put Anna down on the sidewalk and told her to run as fast as she could to try to get back to Felipe's. He reckoned it was less than a mile away, and she'd always had a good sense of direction, although he knew that this was asking a great deal of a young child. But he had no choice.

The ICE official grabbed Carlos by the elbow and asked, at gunpoint, for his papers. When Carlos could only show his Guatemalan identification, the agent told the fugitive that he had to go with him to the station. He placed Carlos in handcuffs and led him toward the ICE vehicle. As they approached the van, Carlos saw the female officer return empty-handed and he was glad that Isabella had escaped ICE's clutches, at least for now. He noted that the woman looked carefully inside the shrine as she passed but did not remove anything.

Carlos was glad that Isabella had escaped, at least for now. At least she might have a chance to stay and be reunited with Anna. He knew his fate was to be sent back to Guatemala and certain death.

Isabella had taken off like a rocket. She turned several times to make sure she lost her pursuer. Fortunately, she was in good shape and wasn't burdened with the heavy uniform, boots, and the Sig Sauer P320 semiautomatic pistol issued to ICE operatives. After ten minutes or so, she slowed to a walk, looking back to confirm that, indeed, she was no longer being followed. She needed to get her bearings, though, and figure out what to do next.

Isabella decided her best option was to try to go back to Felipe's. Really, there was no other choice, even though that was fraught with danger. If Carlos didn't get away, eventually he would have to tell the ICE agents about his brother, and then they would stake out the house to keep an eye on comings and goings. But if he did manage to escape, for sure he would head to his brother's. That was her only chance to be reunited with him and Anna. She didn't know anyone else in East Los Angeles, let alone the United States. The alternative would be to give herself up to ICE, and then from what Felipe had told them, she would be sent back to Guatemala, alone or with Carlos.

Anna had run as fast as the wind, and when she finally dared to glance back, she did not see her father or any pursuers. As her heart regained a normal beat, she started to think what her next step should be. Her father had said to try to go back to Felipe's place, but, as she thought about which way to go, she started to panic. She had no clue. She fought back the tears but remembered that at the little altar she had she'd told her parents she was a grownup now. And she knew crying wouldn't help.

In the end, Anna decided her best bet would be to get back to the shrine where she'd last seen her parents and try to find her way to her uncle's from there. But even locating the concrete wall proved to be a real struggle. It took her the rest of the day, with many twists and turns, hesitations, and stops to wipe away tears before she came upon the makeshift altar. The sky was already growing dark, but she was so happy to see Godfredo and Esperanza, she hugged them both and snuggled with them, notwithstanding what she had said to her parents. She even had a little cry, wiping her tears on the fur of the toy animals. Only afterwards did she munch on a slice of the bread and an apple the teddies had not touched. Then she lay down with the bears and when the moon and stars came out, fell asleep.

As evening fell, Isabella finally dared to approach her brother-in-law's house. Once she had found her way back, she had thought it best to wait and make sure Felipe and Selena were at home, and the home wasn't being watched by the authorities. She pressed the bell several times, and when they answered, she slipped quickly inside and shut the door. Amid tears and hugs, she told them what had happened and asked if Anna and Carlos had come back or gotten in touch.

As Isabella wiped away the tears, Selena sat her down at the kitchen table and, over a bowl of *Pepian,* the traditional Guatemalan meat and vegetable stew, they considered how to proceed. Thinking long and hard, Felipe said he would contact the ICE office the next morning to ask after Carlos and Anna without giving away Isabella's whereabouts. She should stay away from the house during the day in case Carlos told the authorities that he had a brother living in East Los Angeles.

In the morning, after eating an orange left for Godfredo and Esperanza, and giving the tear-dampened teddies each a big hug, Anna set out to find Felipe's residence. But with all the excitement of the last few days, she had very little recollection of what their home looked like and certainly no notion about where it might be located. She walked miles and miles, and stopped in front of numerous houses, but didn't dare knock on any door.

Tired and dejected, in the early evening, she made her way back to the shrine, but decided that perhaps it was not such a good idea to hang around too close to it, since the government agents had found them there and might come by again. She found a cozy sheltered spot under a tree across the boulevard from where she could still see the altar beyond the cracked sidewalk and patches of brown grass. She would try to find Felipe's again the next day, casting a wider net and trying different streets, but for the moment, this would be her home.

When Felipe went to the Department of Homeland Security office on East Olympic Boulevard, he was told that Carlos was in custody and would be deported as soon as his case could be processed. They had no knowledge of Carlos' daughter or wife, and if they came anywhere near his house, it was Felipe's duty to report them.

He went back home and told Isabella, who cried. She worried that Anna was out there, somewhere, still roaming the streets all alone Although upset that her husband would be sent back, she resolved to find her daughter, and knew she had to stay out of ICE's clutches to do so. She could certainly not go to the authorities for help. Felipe offered to lend her his car—perhaps she would get lucky and come upon Anna wandering the streets.

For two days Isabella drove around in ever-widening circles, frequently passing by the shrine. She was at her wits end and in tears with apprehension when she returned empty-handed to her brother-in-law's each evening. Felipe and Selena put out feelers in the Latino community, asking if anyone had seen a little girl in a red dress. They, too, drew a blank.

Anna set out each morning from her little spot near the altar to roam the streets in an effort to find Felipe's. But, as the rations left for the teddies on that blissful day of their thanksgiving disappeared, she was getting more and more despondent and at a loss as to what to do. On the morning of the third day, just as she was trying to figure out what course of action to take, a car pulled up beside the concrete wall. She perked up, hoping against hope that it might be her mother, but thinking that it could also be those agents. She tried hard but could not see the driver's face. Then her view was completely blocked by a huge moving van stopping behind a line of vehicles at the traffic light. When the truck finally moved forward, the car was still there—but where was the driver? She stood up to try to peek around the vehicle.

Isabella knelt in front of the altar and adjusted the burned-out candles. As she looked around the little shrine, she was surprised that the food left for the teddies was gone. Her first thought was that Anna had returned and, very hungry, eaten the bread and fruit. But then again, it was more likely that stray dogs or a homeless person had devoured the offerings. Tears started to flow. She and her little daughter had no home. Worse, Anna was on the streets all alone, mother- and fatherless. She simply had to find her.

Before she stood up, she said one quick prayer for her husband and daughter. Then, on an impulse, she grabbed Godfredo and went quickly back to the car parked illegally on the side of the road. At least she would have the teddy Anna had brought all the way from home to console her. As she held the furry stuffed animal to her face, she could still feel the moistness and smell, the essence of her daughter's tears, imparted over the years. She resolved to be back with more food as soon as she could find a grocery store, just in case Anna was the one who had eaten the little they had left in the altar.

Standing on the other side of the boulevard, Anna could not believe her eyes. Her mother was in that car! Overjoyed, she ran toward the curb yelling, "Mama! Mama!" But the traffic was heavy, and before she could make it across, she saw her mother's vehicle move into the lane and drive away. Anna collapsed on the dilapidated sidewalk and cried.

Minutes passed before she could gather the strength to cross to the shrine. Her mother had taken Godfredo. Did that mean that she had given up for good and would not come back? Her tears started again as she hugged Esperanza, desperate to gain comfort from the softness of Victoria's furry toy animal. And not knowing what to do, she lay down, closed her eyes, and cuddled with the teddy.

She only opened them when she felt someone nudging her. But no, it was not her mother; she recoiled as she saw the smiling blond woman in a uniform with *ICE* written in big white letters. The agent asked, "Where is the other teddy, my dear?" It was only then that Anna realized this must have been the agent who chased her mother. Although she regretted it immediately, she blurted out, "Mama took Godfredo."

The woman then asked where her mother was. Anna had to answer that she didn't know. "Well, you can't stay here," the woman said. "Why don't you just come along with me. What is your name, little girl?"

It took Isabella twenty minutes to find a grocery store where she could park, so by the time she got back to the shrine, almost an hour had elapsed. She hurried to get out of the car with the loaf of sliced bread, fruit and cheese, and saw that Esperanza was gone. Had Anna come back and taken the little toy animal? Or had some other girl? A homeless mother, for her child? Her hands shook as she rummaged around hoping to find a note or a sign. Nothing. Panic overcame her. She was struck with dread that she might never see her daughter again. Or was her mind playing tricks?

The blond ICE agent escorted Anna to the Department of Homeland Security office and left her alone for an eternity in a room with only a table and several chairs. Eventually, the woman and a man in a white shirt with rolled-up sleeves and a loosened tie came and asked her a few questions. She told them yes, Carlos de Leon was her father, and that she had not seen either of her parents since the day the agents gave chase. She just wanted to be together with them again, she added in tears. The officials looked at each other, then the man, in heavily accented Spanish, said, "That won't be possible. Your father already signed the Separated Parent's Removal Form. He's being sent back to Guatemala without you. And we're still looking for your mother."

Several hours later, the blond woman came back and told Anna to come along with her. She and the male agent drove her to a detention center where she again had to answer many questions. The ICE operatives left, and a stern woman dressed in blue overalls told her this would be her home for now. Then she led Anna down a long austere corridor to a room where lots of children were eating soup and sandwiches. Since she was very hungry, she joined in, although it was hard to keep back the tears whenever she thought about all that had happened in the last few days.

She missed her parents desperately and, hugging Esperanza tightly, she longed for Godfredo. What would happen to her now? And where was her mother? What had happened to her? Oh, and her poor father—would she ever see him again?

Isabella drove as fast as she could back to Felipe's. She needed to talk things over with him and Selena. She had come to depend on their counsel. Felipe told her that he would go back to the Department of Homeland Security office to find out what he could about Carlos and Anna. He would simply ask after his relatives, one of whom he knew was in their custody. The problem, he told her, was that since they had entered illegally, Carlos would be deported. As would she, if she were caught. But they could opt for Anna to stay in the USA, and she, as a minor, would more than likely be granted asylum, especially if he and Selena sponsored her. Which, of course, they would.

Felipe thought that Isabella should just disappear. They would help her find a place nearby to live, and he and Selena would bring Anna home to live with them. At least that way, Anna could become legal. Eventually, a path might open up for Isabella to get her papers and perhaps bring Carlos to the US. Provided the gang didn't get his poor brother before then back in Guatemala—but this, Felipe kept to himself.

The next day, the Department of Homeland Security official told Felipe that Anna De Leon had been found and was in a detention center. The authorities were now seeking her mother, and had her father in custody, waiting to be deported. Carlos had already signed the Separated Parent's Removal Form, so they would send him back without Anna. Felipe told the authorities that he and his wife would be happy to sponsor his niece as an underage migrant refugee. The man explained that he would need to go with his wife to the Office of Refugee Resettlement to start the process.

That evening, Felipe told Isabella everything. He and Selena would do whatever was needed to be approved as sponsors for Anna. In the meantime, they had some friends close by who would put Isabella up. It wasn't safe for her at their place—the authorities knew they were her only contacts in the USA. For Carlos, alas, they could do nothing, although he would consult an immigration lawyer just in case.

It took more than a month for Anna to be released to Felipe and Selena's loving care. During the stay in the detention center, away from parents and relatives, she had become less talkative, more withdrawn, and would not, under any circumstances, part with Esperanza. When Felipe picked her up, he was shocked by how thin and traumatized the little girl was—clearly, not being sure whether her mother was still alive and knowing she might never see her father again were psychologically devastating.

Anna did perk up a bit when they returned home. She seemed comforted by being cuddled and spoiled by Selena and Victoria. But when later that evening, they took her over to where Isabella was staying and she was reunited with her mother, at least for the moment, everyone's tears of joy washed away, all the pain and suffering of the last couple of months. When Isabella brought out Godfredo, Anna's happiness was almost complete—if only her father could join them!

The parting that evening was very difficult, and only eased by Godfredo leaving with Anna, and promises that they would be together very soon. But Felipe knew they would have to tread carefully: the agents from ICE were, no doubt, still wanting to get their hands on the illegal Isabella to deport her. And that would be tragic, not just for Anna, but likely for all of them.

They did come, the ICE agents. The blond woman and her male partner who had originally given chase showed up at Felipe's house a few weeks later, on one of their surprise calls. Isabella was fortunately not there, but they found Anna hugging the larger teddy. The female agent asked Anna whether this was Godfredo and if her mother had brought him back to her. Anna broke down in tears.

Selena intervened and told the ICE agent to leave the girl alone. The other agent then threatened Anna's aunt: he explained in harsh words that harboring an illegal immigrant was a criminal offense, and even though she and her husband held green cards, they could be deported. Either they divulged where Isabella was, or ICE would start criminal proceedings. Felipe came home to find his wife and niece in tears with Anna desperately hugging Godfredo, as the two agents searched the house, certain that Isabella had given the male teddy bear back to Anna and hoping to find the illegal Guatemalan woman on the premises.

Just then, Victoria and Jorge came home from their extracurricular activities. Felipe asked them to take their cousin outside to play and told the ICE agents that he wanted to be alone with his wife for a few minutes. They retired to their bedroom, and then into the bathroom, where Felipe turned the shower on to prevent the agents from hearing their conversation.

They had no choice, Felipe concluded, but to give Isabella up, terrible as that seemed. For if they, too, were deported, all three children would lose their adult relatives. This way, at least, they would be able to raise Anna with their two and give her a safe and decent life. He was sure that was what Carlos and Isabella would want. Reluctantly, Selena agreed.

Back in the room with the agents, Felipe asked if they could talk to his sister-in-law and if Anna could see her mother. The male agent said, "You must be joking! Mister, my patience is running out." And then he again demanded the address where Isabella was hiding. Felipe said he would divulge it provided the people who were putting her up wouldn't suffer any consequences. The agent said, "No promises. They're also committing a crime."

When the children came back inside, Felipe could tell from the way she looked at him that Anna sensed what had happened. She was crying, hugging Godfredo, and mumbling, "I want my Mama," and "I want my Papa," between sobs.

It took many months of loving care for Selena and Felipe to bring Anna out of the hopeless depression she fell into when her mother did not come, day in, day out. Nor did her father. Godfredo and Esperanza helped, as did Victoria and Jorge. And, eventually, school, and making friends, living a more or less normal life . . . If growing up without your father and mother could ever be called that.

* * *

Years later, Felipe found out through the Guatemalan grapevine that Carlos and Isabella had arrived back in their country separately on the flights run by the US government to return deported asylum seekers. Carlos was murdered by the Mara Salvatrucha gang soon after. Isabella disappeared into the underworld of prostitution and sex slavery.

Anna would never see her parents again. Her only reminder of home for the rest of her life was her little bear. To this day, she keeps Godfredo and Esperanza propped up on a bookshelf in the living room of her home to remind her of who she was, and how she came to the USA with her parents.

But she no longer wipes her tears on the teddies' fur.

The Veteran and the Passerby

He was always just standing there, on the corner, down by the parking lot, whenever I went to Safeway. Always tanned, thin, but once obviously very fit, with longish hair and piercing blue eyes. On sunny days, in filthy shorts, a torn T-shirt and flip-flops. When colder, in dirty jeans and a tattered Grateful Dead hoodie. A beige, paint-speckled red backpack, presumably holding his meager possessions, placed carelessly in the dirt against the tree in the corner of the lot. His greasy Giants baseball cap upside down, right there, down on the sidewalk by his always moving feet, a few coins and crumpled dollar bills thrown in, crying out for companions to skip across the void and join them from the pockets of passersby like me.

One of San Francisco's homeless, for sure, I told myself. In unusual territory, though—most hang out down in the Tenderloin area and not in the swanky Marina. Looks like a veteran, too. Iraq, maybe? Or Afghanistan?

Who is this fucker anyway? This weird guy who always looks me over, this pervert who stares at me as he goes by? First, with his nerdish backpack, all floppy and empty, slung over one shoulder. Thinks he is so fucking nonchalant, the asshole does. Then, eons later, on his way back, rucksack filled to the brim—with groceries, rocks, turds or whatever— so that the motherfucker looks like he's struggling to lug the weight of the world on his shoulders. Like Jesus Christ carrying the fucking cross on his way to Golgotha or something. Shit, this guy would've never made it over in the Sandpit, that's a given, wearing battle rattle and all—the weight alone would have killed the sucker in a sec. The Hajis would have downed him for sure, first time out. I tell you . . .

Jake—for that is what he told me he was called when one day I'd finally asked his name after he grunted a thanks for the dollar bill I dropped into the cap—was always chatting away, mumbling something *sotto voce.* Who knew about what and why, but I heard the low muttering often enough on my trips to the grocery store, so that one Friday morning when Marcia was looking after the grandkids and I had nothing pressing on my agenda, on the spur of the moment, I decided, why not talk to the guy, see what he has to say for himself. So I invited Jake for a coffee at Starbucks just up the street. He was rather taken aback by the invitation, but seemed okay with it, maybe a bit torn at first though, since he would have to relinquish his usual spot for a while, but the prospect of a coffee and possibly something to fill the stomach was too tantalizing to refuse.

And now the a-hole is saying something to me—what the fuck? He's asking me if I want to go to Starbucks with him. Says he'll buy me a coffee. Is he making a pass at me, the queer geezer? Well, maybe no harm, I can certainly handle the fucker if he tries to suck me off. At least I will get a cup of joe and a muffin out of it. Haa! But no blow job for him . . .

I ordered a large coffee with milk and lots of sugar and a blueberry muffin for Jake, a cappuccino for myself. We sat down at a corner table, putting our twin backpacks at our feet. He held his paper cup with both hands, slowly slurping the hot liquid through the lid, occasionally glancing up at me.

"Thanks, man," he finally blurted out, breaking the silence between us. I sensed real gratitude there. From the way he looked at me, it seemed that this was the first time in a while anyone had invited him for coffee. Or for anything.

"No problem, Jake," I answered, pleased. Then after a pause, while our eyes met, "Where are you from?"

Jesus, he just won't let up with the questions, will he, the fucker? I already told him my name—not my real one, of course—and now he wants to know where I'm from. Christ, what the fuck for? Jesus, this is like being questioned by fucking al Qaeda—you know, name, rank and serial number—just before they beat the holy living shit outta you.

Of course, Jake gave me an inane answer—that now he was just from here. I left it at that and rather asked him as nonchalantly as I could, "So, I'm intrigued, Jake. Why do you stand on that corner down by Safeway every day?"

So now the cocksucker, he wants to know why I stand where I stand whenever I want to. And if it's every fucking day, so what? Well, fuck nuts, isn't it obvious? Because it's a good place to watch dick fingers like you march past and stare at me. And, just maybe, to collect a few coins from all you greedy capitalist pigs.

Jake looked at me as if I was plain stupid, without deigning to give me an answer.

I let silence rule while he munched on his muffin. "So, Jake,"—I wanted to probe what had happened to the guy, but by this time, I was ready to believe that this, too, might be futile—"where were you stationed? Will you tell me what happened over there? May I ask, Jake—do you have PTSD?"

There, I finally got the question out, the one I'd been wanting to ask my coffee companion all along.

Shit, man! The dude now wants to know what happened . . . what the fuck for? Whether I have PTSD . . . of course, you asshole, can't you see? Can't you fucking TELL?

I could see that this set of questions did not sit well, because Jake took a big gulp of his coffee and then just sat there, eyes vacant, looking into his cup, not saying anything. But I thought there was something going on in that mind of his, though I wasn't entirely sure.

Okay, you jerk off, Stan—or whatever the fuck you said your name was. I'll tell you what happened. Of course, you and all the other little pricks and cunts we went over there for will never really know what it was like when we were out in the red zone. Whatever I might be able to tell you here in fucking Cow Hollow will pale compared to what the reality actually was.

Jake's mien had suddenly taken on an angry, almost vicious, character.

And never mind, all the killing and maiming that went on before the straw that broke the camel's back (motherfucker, excuse the sick, sandy pun). The semblance of a smile had appeared on his face. *You sort of get inured to it after a while. Although, progressively, the horror of it all builds up, weighs on you—not you, asshole, because you never went. But we were fucking there to do a job. We were there to kill or be killed.*

I could see that Jake's lips were moving—or perhaps trembling—but nothing audible came out. He just kept staring ahead without looking at anything.

Okay, ass licker, what finally did me in happened three weeks before the end of my second tour. My two best buddies and I—we were out looking for IEDs—jerk off, that's short for improvised explosive devices—because the fucking Hajis would stick them all over so that we would knock against them or step on them. They just tried to shove them up our collective ass, they did, wherever we were. Finding these gizmos was laborious work, and you had to sort of do it by feel. And unless you sensed one, smelled it or used fucking ESP to ferret it out, you were likely to be blown to smithereens.

So, my two mates, Bob and Will, were doing this excruciating job while I was a few paces behind monitoring three-sixty for the fucking Muj. Yeah, the shit asses would come out of nowhere and fucking do a death blossom that was sure to blow your head off if you were in the way. Will, who had just started his first tour in the Sandbox and didn't have a shitload of experience, fucking poked the sand with his HK G3—and BAM! A bloody mega-explosion right in front of me. I hit the dirt, went under, unconscious.

Jake's hands suddenly flew up in the air and from his eyes I could now see that he was getting worked up, but still no sound emanated from his mouth.

"Jake, it's all right," I said, as I looked around, not wanting him to make a scene. "You don't need to tell me if you don't want to."

Fuck, man! Just shut up and listen, for God's sake. I don't know how long I was out, but it couldn't have been more than a few minutes, because a wildfire was still raging right in front of me when I came to. I had gone stone deaf, could not hear a fucking thing. I slowly pulled myself together, a few bruises here and there, my left arm lacerated, bleeding badly. I ripped off what was left of my battle rattle, got down to my undershirt, which I just tore off my shaking body and used it to bandage what was fucking left of my arm.

Then I looked around.

Across the table from me, Jake seemed to be favoring his left arm, holding it with his right hand. He swiveled his head as if to check out the neighboring tables—maybe he thought he was making a spectacle of himself. Then his eyes went to the floor as if he had dropped something. His face contorted in a terrified grimace.

My buddies were nowhere. I looked again, down low. Strewn around all over the fucking desert were body parts. A bleeding hand still twitching, a boot with part of a calf protruding, tendons and bloody flesh and all, half of what may have been Will's head, just red meat, brains, hair and blood all over, including, as I looked again at myself, on me. I blinked, hoping the horror scene would go away . . . and puked my insides out, right there in the fucking sand. When I got up from my knees, I was shaking and bawling like I hadn't since I was a babe—for fuck's sake, Will was just a child. He still carried a picture of his mom! And Bob, he was the joker in the crew, a fucking strongman. Both dead. Fucking blown to bits.

I looked at Jake, puzzled, as tears welled in his eyes, one dropping on the lid of his cup.

Here one second, pulp the next.

From dust to dust. The only thing fucking religion ever got right. I tell you.

When I had no more tears to shed, I realized there was nothing I could do for my buddies, so I did another three-sixty scan, looked around in the sand to see if any of our weapons were still intact, and seeing this was hopeless, started hightailing it back the best I could toward where I thought the FOB was—the Forward Operating Base, you anal pore. In retrospect, I know some would say I was goddam lucky, because within what seemed like only moments, a gun truck pulled up and two of our grunts jumped out and fucking hoisted me in, lock, stock and barrel. I vaguely remember them telling me before I passed out they'd heard the blast and got there as soon as they could.

Jake wiped his eyes with his sleeves before taking another sip of his coffee.

I came to, sometime later back at the FOB on a hospital cot. Noticed my arm was all bandaged up. Doctor came over in a little while, told me my arm would be okay, asked me a few questions—my hearing was still not a hundred per cent—but I knew he was fucking assessing me. He told me I would be sent home on the next transport.

I was angry, because, fuck, I just wanted to get out there again and shoot up as many Haji as I could before I went home. To avenge Will and Bob. And all the others. When the doctor left, I climbed out of bed and tried to make my way out of the shithole of a hospital to get my hands on any kind of a submachine gun or grenade launcher, even though my fucking arm would have made it difficult to operate one of these. Two cock-sucking male nurses grabbed me, though, took me back to the cot and said I'd better stay put or they would have to put me in the cage.

The next day, they let me go back to the barracks to await transfer back home the following week. But, sure as hell, I was not going to fucking lie on my cot and just beat off all day. There were enough arms around in the room, some of my buddies' automatics, so . . .

All of a sudden Jake jumped up from his seat and started

acting like he was shooting an imaginary machinegun. I grabbed him by the elbow, scooped up the two backpacks with the other hand, and led him out to the sidewalk.

"Jake, my friend, are you alright?" I asked, shaking him by the shoulders.

It took him a moment or two to recover and pull himself out of what must have been some kind of a trance, reliving a horrific experience. Then, with a grimace, he slowly answered, "Yes, Stan."

"Are you sure? What was going on there?"

Fuck. Not again. The dude wants to know what I . . . never fucking mind.

After a long pause, during which he stared blankly into my eyes, Jake said, "Thanks for the coffee, mate. See you around. Down by Safeway. Maybe."

I watched him shuffle slowly down the hill in his flip-flops, shaking his head and muttering something.

* * *

The next morning, a Saturday, Marcia and I were having a late breakfast after a night out on the town with friends. Just as I was taking our soft-boiled eggs out of the boiling water, a deafening blast shook the building. It penetrated my whole being, so I knew it couldn't have come from very far away. We looked at each other. I muttered, "What the . . ." And then we hurried outside up to a spot where I could "scan three-sixty," as Jake had said. Our attention went immediately over to where there was a huge pillar of black smoke rising high in the sky and where all the sirens seemed to be focusing. About a mile away, I guessed. And then it hit me: that was where Safeway was.

"Let's get over there," I said. "I want to go see what happened." Of course, I was concerned for my coffee mate.

Marcia was a little dubious, although I was the one who usually tried to avoid potential hotspots, but she came along.

When we got near, we saw that the police had cordoned off

the site. Where the Safeway had been was now a gaping hole. Flames leaped up here and there from what remained of our local grocery store. I looked around to see if Jake was in his usual spot, but that corner, too, had been blown away, and lay well within the cordoned area.

"Excuse me, sir," I addressed one of the policemen teeming around the site. "Can you tell us what happened?"

"Well, it seems a bomb was detonated at Safeway less than an hour ago."

"Any idea of who did it? And why?"

"Nope," the officer responded. "I doubt we'll ever know for sure."

* * *

Back home, we turned on the TV, clicked through CNN, then the local stations. Eventually, news of the event came on: ". . . officials are still not sure of the death toll in the tragic bombing at a Safeway in San Francisco today." They zoomed in on a picture I recognized.

"At least a hundred people might have been there on such a fine Saturday morning, a Safeway spokeswoman told us. It will take some time for authorities to get a handle on the number of casualties. Police still have no idea of what caused the blast—forensic experts are combing over the site. Was it an accident? An act of terrorism? If so, who did it, and why? These are the questions the authorities hope to find answers to over the next several days."

* * *

The days passed, and officialdom concluded, based on some forensic evidence, that it likely was a bombing, some kind of homemade bomb. An IED—improvised explosive device—Jake had called it.

Each morning, I wandered over to as close to the spot where Jake used to hang out as I could and walked from there up the hill to Starbucks for my coffee, then back down again to the bombing site. But I never saw my friend again. I even made some discreet inquiries at local hospitals, but a wiry veteran named Jake had not registered anywhere.

He must have perished in the bombing, I lamented to myself. And, when I thought about our coffee at Starbuck's the day before the explosion, in my heart of hearts, I was sure Jake was the tortured being who had planted and detonated the IED.

A homeless veteran who, along with his buddies, had given all for his country, which, in the end, was not there for him.

He took his revenge and frustration out the only way he knew how.

And, to boot, it also ended the searing pain of his memories.

A win-win.

The Phone Number

The door to the container slid open with a loud grating noise. Daylight crept in, assaulting Katya's still-tired eyes. She blinked and raised her head slowly as Eva stirred beside her on the bare mattress and she heard groans and sobs from the other girls who were waking to the sudden sunlight streaming in from outside. First one, then another male silhouette loomed as black shadows against the blinding brightness. As they moved inside, Katya immediately recognized Ivan the driver and then Rick, who seemed to be the contact man.

"You, there," Ivan shouted at someone in the dark over on the other side. "And you two." Now his gaze beckoned Katya. "Come. We need to get you washed and dressed."

And when there was no response from the exhausted girls, Ivan made his way over to their mattress and grabbed Katya by the arm, pulled her up, and shoved her toward the opening before doing the same to Eva.

"Yes, my dear, you have some work to do again this afternoon," Katya heard the rasping voice of the one called Rick, still over by the entrance. "Get your ass over here, babe. You gotta earn your keep, for fuck's sake."

It had been Rick who had recruited her into this terrible mess, masquerading as an agent from the University of Florida offering a very selective scholarship. It had all sounded so, so tempting . . . and stupidly, she had fallen for it.

Katya moved hesitantly toward Rick. He grabbed her as soon as she was within reach and, twisting her arm, tugged her down the ramp toward the little building beside which the container had been parked.

"Okay, you stupid bitch, get inside, and wash up and put some clean clothes on. You'll find everything you need in the hut."

Katya knew she had no choice. If she resisted, the punishment would be hell. Could be serial rape by all four of the minders or hanging naked from a hook in the ceiling of the container all night, on tiptoes, then being abused mentally and physically, or both. But no marks, at least there was that. They wanted to keep the girls intact for the customers.

Or she could end up like Anna, who disappeared after God only knows what they did to her. No, she had to stop thinking about it. She had to go along with what they said for now, but she needed to find a way to escape.

And there was a ray of hope, as of last evening. The phone number. 1-888-373-7888.

Katya had finally fallen asleep the night before as she was going over the telephone number she'd seared in her memory earlier that day when she'd been delivered in a van to a hotel to be with another customer. Right after the creep had maneuvered her into the bedroom, she'd gone to the bathroom on the pretext of needing to empty herself, but really to gain time to think and prepare herself mentally for the horrors that would inevitably come next.

There, beside the granite sink, she'd been surprised to see the piece of soap with the number "1-888-373-7888" and the words *National Human Trafficking Hotline* under it, marked on the wrapper. She had quickly committed the number to memory and flushed the wrapper down the toilet—certainly, she didn't want the beast out there, or worse still, her minders to see it. She delayed for as long as she could in the bathroom to go over the telephone number, but when the pervert started to shake the door, she knew she no longer had any choice.

As she stripped and reluctantly satisfied the brute, Katya hoped that once done, she would have a chance to use the phone by the bedside, or if not, then steal the man's mobile, but there had been no opportunity. Her handlers came promptly, and they and the customer gave her no privacy. They shoved her around and slapped her on the rear before the gangsters whisked her back to the container where the trafficked girls were kept for the duration of the Super Bowl. That night, she whispered the number to Eva, the only girl she trusted now that Anna was gone. Perhaps one of them might find a way to call the hotline.

Yes, that number would be her salvation. She would get to a phone somehow. She simply had to. Maybe today. The sooner the better.

Showered, dressed and made-up, Katya and Eva and a third girl they barely knew—Trish, an American teenager, she thought—were shoved by Ivan and Rick into the back of a white van with no windows. Ivan drove for half an hour, Katya guessed, before they pulled off the road and then, after a few turns, brought the van to a halt.

"God, I hope this won't be as horrible as the last time," Trish whined, barely able to hold back her tears. Outside, they heard Rick greet some men, and after some jovial exchanges they couldn't make out, the van door opened.

"Come on, girls, time to perform," Rick said. "The customers are waiting."

The girls slowly clambered out of the back of the van and into the sunlight. Five men stood there, all with hungry, leering expressions.

"Wow!" Katya heard the smallest pervert utter. "They sure are beauts, just like you said."

"Have fun, you guys," Rick yelled, as he got back in the passenger seat. "We'll pick the girls up in six hours."

A big hulk with his shirt open revealing a hairy chest and a large gut moved toward Katya, grabbed her by the arm and said, "This one's mine. At least I get first dibs."

"No fair, Jeb, we said we would toss a coin."

"Fuck that, Lenny. You should be glad I let you come along. The other two aren't bad, either. And we'll trade later, don't you worry. You'll get your turn, if you can still get it up." A raucous laugh followed.

The man called Jeb twisted Katya's arm behind her and tugged the frightened girl into the luxurious villa, through the beautifully furnished living room, and into a huge bedroom with a king-size bed, whipping her around to face him as he started pawing her. Katya tried to wriggle away, but he tore her blouse and ripped her miniskirt off. Then he whirled her around and shoved her down on the bed.

To put off the agony, as the brute started to undress, Katya turned around and pleaded, "I need to go to the bathroom. Please. Before . . ."

Jeb looked at her with disgust. "Okay, you stupid bitch. But take your bra off first and make it fast."

Katya quickly got up, did as she was told and, covering her breasts as best she could, made her way to the bathroom. Jeb yelled after her, "Don't lock the fucking door, you cunt."

Shaking, she nevertheless pulled the door closed and sat down on the toilet, burying her face in her hands. The terrible thought entered her mind that after Jeb, several other men were waiting to get at her. There were five or six horny revelers to the three girls. Trish and Eva had been coerced into entertaining the others with an erotic dance à *deux* while the hairy bully, this Jeb who had claimed first dibs, would have his way with her.

She thought of the soap and the number, and that gave her strength. Finishing, she gingerly opened the door. The hairy beast, gut hanging over his filthy boxers, grabbed her, twisted her around, and reached down inside her panties. He ripped them off with brute force, then whipped her back around and planted a mouth that reeked of alcohol on hers. She tried to resist but knew full well that there was no way she could avoid what was to come next. As she struggled, Katya glanced around to see if there was a phone anywhere. But Jeb dragged her to the bed and pushed her face-down into the pillows.

"What the fuck were you doing in there for so long, you

stupid Russian cunt?" he yelled. "Playing with your clit? I'll teach you!"

Katya kept reciting 3737 to herself, sure she would remember the 888's on either side, as Jeb forced himself into her from behind and stifled her scream with a sweaty hand over her mouth. She knew she had to endure this horror, live through it as best she could. She tried to think ahead to the aftermath when she would have to find the strength to rummage through the lowlife's clothes for his cellphone—since there didn't seem to be a fixed line in this posh villa, certainly not in this bedroom—just as soon as he released her and hopefully disappeared into the bathroom to wash himself. And it would have to be done very quickly.

Katya was in tears from the pain and humiliation as the fat slob finally finished doing his thing. He slowly got off her, slapping her hard on the buttocks. "Well done, babe." Jeb laughed. "You sure are a great fuck. Even though you are one stupid Russian cunt."

He slid off the bed, looked down at his condom-covered member, picked up his boxers and headed for the bathroom as he chuckled, "Yuck! I guess I'd better wash myself off."

As soon as the monster closed the bathroom door—in spite of the pain she felt down below—Katya got up and started to go through the clothes he'd thrown in a pile on a chair. Sure enough, she found an iPhone in the pants' pocket and hoped it wasn't locked. But just as she was about to check, someone knocked on the bedroom door.

"Hey Jeb, you jerkoff!" She heard a man's voice yell. "What the fuck is taking you so long? Give us other guys a turn." And then, after a pause, "or maybe two of us should do it at the same time, eh? Double tag her. How about it?"

As Jeb flushed the toilet, Katya slid back onto the bed and shoved the mobile under the mattress. She tried to assume the same position she had been in before, all the time continuing to sob, but managed to pull the duvet over her aching body. As she did so, she noticed the blood down the back of her thighs and on the sheets. Sure enough, Jeb lumbered over to the bedroom door and as he unlocked it, Katya hoped he wouldn't notice that his clothes had been gone through or that his phone was gone. If he did, that would be the end of her.

"Well, well, so you horny guys want to have a turn with this cunt, do you?" Jeb said, opening the door wide. "I guess I'm done with her for now. Do come in, do come in."

"Jeb, fuck it. You can't just monopolize the best babe in town, you dickhead. You can bet your fat ass we want to have a go."

"Yeah, this one is a hottie all right." Jeb yanked the duvet off, exposing Katya to the others.

The guy at the door yelled back into the living room, "Hey, who wants to do a duo with the hot blonde chick Jeb just made?"

Someone shouted back, "With you, Bob, you shithead? Not on your life . . ." as another partyer appeared.

"Jesus, Jeb, why the fuck don't you get her to wash herself? She's got your scum and sweat all over her bod—and is that blood down there? What the fuck did you do to her, you asshole? I ain't goin' near the bitch until she washes."

"Did you hear what my friend said—what the fuck's your name—Katya? Get up and go wash yourself. And don't close the door, because we all want to watch."

Katya just lay there not moving, thinking this time disobedience might be her best strategy. Besides, she was glad to be immobile. That way, the pain was more or less tolerable.

"Shit, Jeb." Bob came closer to the bed. "Did you fucking kill the twat?" He grabbed her wrist. "Well, at least she has a pulse. Maybe we just need to let her rest a mo. Let's go and play with the other two babes."

The three slobs left the room, but they left the door open a crack. Katya did not move as she listened to the sounds from the other room, glad to be left alone.

"Come on, baby," she heard from afar one of the men say a moment later, "it's time for blow jobs all around! Both of you, come on, show us what you can do with your fucking lips and tongues."

"Yeah, great stuff!" Katya heard Bob say. "Get your ass over here, Eva, and get on it."

She tried to close her ears to this disgusting banter and the sounds, and concentrate on her next move. She figured she would have maybe fifteen minutes—maybe one or two more—if all the men were going to join in whatever was going on next door.

Katya felt around under the mattress. As soon as her right hand locked on the phone, she maneuvered her body out of the bed as gently and as quietly as possible. She moved quickly to the lavatory, holding the cell between her breasts and away from the door to the living room. Katya closed the bathroom door quietly, latching it so the brutes would have to break it down to get to her. She sat on the toilet, opened the phone . . . and was devastated when she saw that it needed a pin number or a thumbprint. The realization that she would not be able to call the National Trafficking Hotline at 1-888-3737888 brought her to tears. But then, at the bottom of the screen she noticed the word *Emergency*. With her shaking finger, she pressed that corner and put the phone to her ear, hoping this would work.

A reassuring female voice came on the line with an urgent, "911, what's your emergency?"

When Katya didn't say anything, the woman continued, "Please, can you tell me what is wrong? Where are you?"

"I am somewhere . . . big house . . . in bathroom. We are being trafficked . . . horribly abused. Two other girls. We were brought here to have . . . sex with awful men."

"What is your name?"

"Katya . . . Gusov."

"Who else is in the house, Katya?"

"Eva Baransky. And . . . Trish . . . I don't know name. Six men . . . terrible men. We brought here by gang . . . they brought us from Florida . . . in truck. They rent us for sex to these men. These . . . perverts . . . do horrible things. Please . . ."

"Katya, is there anything else you can tell us to help us find the house?"

"It is, I think, rented. Some villa . . . pretty . . . how do you say it . . . posh. Other times we kept in container by gang. Maybe . . . twenty-five minutes or half an hour from here. They bring us here in van. These men already at villa. Oh, please help us!"

"Katya, I know this is dangerous for you, but you need to keep talking to me for just a little longer. We are trying to locate where you are and every second helps. Now, do you know any names?"

"Just Jeb, I think," Katya said between sobs. "And there is Bob and . . . I don't know . . ."

A scream penetrated through the two doors. Katya wondered what those animals were doing to Eva and Trish.

"Please, please, hurry! I am so afraid . . . I must put cell phone back in man's pockets now . . . I took it from pants he left on chair."

"Katya, you mention the gang . . . did the men who brought you here . . . did they have an accent?"

"Yes, some did. Russian. They spoke to me in Russian. Some others American . . ."

"Okay, Katya, you've done great . . . we have a pinpoint. We're on our way. Hold out just a little longer, dear."

Katya was shaking as she turned the mobile off. She grabbed a tissue to wipe the tears from her eyes, quickly washed herself, and quietly opened the door. She listened a moment to the sounds emanating from the living room—moaning and groaning, grunting and panting, an occasional slap followed by a whimper or a scream. She rapidly made her way over to the chair where Jeb's clothes were in a messy pile, and, with hands shaking, put the phone back in the pocket where she had found it.

As Katya was collecting what was left of her torn clothes, she heard Bob say, "Hey, it seems your cunt is finally back in the world of the living, Jeb. I just heard some noises from next door."

"Well, let's get her in here to join in the fun. We haven't seen what the bitch can do with those beautiful lips of hers, have we, guys? Her ass certainly was quite something." Jeb let out a raucous laugh.

Katya recoiled as she heard a high-pitched squeak say, "I'll go get her." She quickly ran back toward the bathroom.

"Okay, Lenny. It's probably your turn, anyway."

The little man called Lenny appeared in the bedroom just as Katya slammed the bathroom door shut and locked it. She leaned against it, slumped to the floor and curled into a fetal position. "No, no. No, please no."

From the other side, she heard Lenny yell, "Hey, the bitch just locked herself in the fucking bathroom."

"Well, break the door down, you idiot." This from Jeb.

"Yeah, we can't let her get away with it. The stupid cunt has only put out for Jeb. We got to get our fucking money's worth," another man shouted and entered the fray.

"Okay, okay. I'll see what I can do." Lenny slammed his shoulder into the door and Katya could feel it rattle and shake. But it held. She needed it to hold until the police came.

"Shit! The fucking thing is solid."

"Okay, okay. You pussy. I'll come in a second," Jeb grumbled. "You're useless anyway, you little cunt."

Katya heard someone fall with a cry. Probably Trish, by far the youngest of the girls.

"You have no tits and no butt," Jeb said. "And you just can't move your fucking lips fast enough. We're gonna get our money back, for sure."

"Come on, Jeb."

"Okay, Lenny, let's both put our shoulders to this fucking door. One, two, three . . . ho."

The door gave a little. But it held.

"Again!"

It still held.

"Fuck!" Jeb shouted, sounding really pissed off. "Come on, Lenny, let's really do it."

This time the doorjamb broke. The two slobs came crashing through the opening. Lenny fell on top of Katya where she was against the far wall, trembling. As Jeb recovered and pulled her out from under his buddy, he said, "Come on, babe, it's time for you to service little Lenny here. And my other friends next door."

Back in the bedroom, the weasel called Lenny pulled his

member out and started working it as Jeb forced Katya to her knees in front of him, tearing her already shredded T-shirt off again.

At that very moment, there was a loud crash, as one of the picture windows in the living room was smashed to smithereens and a posse of cops in full battle gear broke through and pointed automatics at the men in the midst of their lewd activities. Two of the policemen appeared at the bedroom door and Jeb let go of Katya, with one hand. She flopped to the floor as one of the cops yelled, "Okay, don't anybody move! Let the girl go."

Lenny, with his boxers down at his ankles, said, "Oh, no!"

Jeb just said, "Shit!"

As they both raised their hands, Katya gingerly stood up and, covering her breasts with her arms, moved toward the police while glancing back at her tormentors. "Thank you. Thank you," were the only words she could utter to the police as she was overwhelmed by her tears—of pain, of suffering, of humiliation but mostly of relief.

"You're safe now, honey," Katya heard a policewoman say from the door to the living room. "Come, sit here beside your friend." Still trembling, she went over to the couch and hugged a weeping, bruised, and naked Eva. The female agent found a blanket somewhere and helped the girls cover themselves. Still unable to shed her fear, Katya watched as Jeb and Lenny and the other perverts were handcuffed and led to the police cars outside. Slowly though, she felt the warmth of hope envelope her, hope that her ordeal as a trafficked woman was over.

Many young women worldwide are trafficked for sex by ruthless gangs. Major sports events that attract male fans, like the Super Bowl, World Cup, the Olympics, and top golf and tennis competitions, are prime venues for traffickers to carry out their sordid business. To fight human trafficking, some public and civic groups have mounted a widespread effort focusing especially on such sports events to promote the National Human Trafficking Hotline (1-888-373-7888).

The line was created and is operated in the USA by Polaris, a nonprofit, nongovernmental entity.

These efforts have included the placement of bars of soap and makeup wipes with the number on the wrapper in hotel bathrooms, as well as the distribution and placement of cards and posters in hotel lobbies. They have had good success, resulting in nearly 276,654 contacts through 2019. A similar hotline was implemented in Canada by the Canadian Centre to End Human Trafficking in 2019. Most cellphones now have a feature so that emergency calls can be placed free of charge from anywhere without the need to unlock the phone.

This short story is a humble effort to help publicize the hotline and to illustrate graphically the lifesaving benefits these measures are having.

Part II

DREAMING

These stories are based on dreams I captured by writing them down, most of them some time ago. I worked these into full-fledged short stories, partly to show the contrast between how the creative process works as we dream, versus when we create fiction in a fully conscious mental state, but primarily because I was fascinated by them. I hope the reader will share this delight.

The Crossing

I knew it was time to go home. The angle of the shadows cast by the slender concrete and glass skyscrapers across the enormous, sterile plaza told me that it was already late. From my squatting position near the middle of the square, I glanced one last time at the few objects arrayed haphazardly in front of me: the pocketknife, the handkerchief, the two smooth pebbles. My only remaining belongings. I'd scattered these in a vain attempt to create disharmony in the frustrating order of the cubist pattern fabricated by the pink and purple stone tiles of the piazza. I frowned involuntarily. No, I was not happy with the result, the arrangement I had created. Disappointed with another wasted afternoon, I expelled a sigh and stood to gather up my possessions, stuffing them one-by-one into the pockets of my tight-fitting shorts.

I started toward where I subconsciously seemed to know that a grassy slope descended to the river. Along the way, I amused myself by playing hopscotch atop the huge stone slabs. As I neared the water, I sensed that the topography immediately in front of me was somewhat familiar. A scene, *déjà vu*, perhaps from my youth? Was the river at the bottom of the incline the Danube, then? Could this be the very same waterway I had grown up near? It didn't really matter much, I comforted myself: I knew that I had to cross it, for home lay on the other side.

At long last, I arrived at the edge of the plaza. I hooted with delight like a chimpanzee when I saw the newly mown grass leading down to the water. Checking my pockets to make sure that my personal effects were secure, I folded my arms across my chest, lay on my side right at the edge of the lawn, and propelled myself, like a misshapen log down the hillside. Only when my descent came to an abrupt and painful halt on the gravel path at the bottom and I started to assume a sitting position again, did I realize how costly this act of indulgence had been. I would now have to climb back up the slope, for it was only from the top that one had access to the suspension bridge.

Doggedly, I set out. The ascent was tough going and I cursed my foolish lack of prudence. Halfway up the hill, I stopped to catch my breath, rationalizing the rest with the need to assess the remaining climb still in front of me. Looking up at the bridge, I decided it would be smarter actually to take a shortcut by scrambling up to, and across, one of the massive steel suspension cables, rather than go all the way around to where the road from the plaza emptied onto the bridge. These cables—really, girders—took me back in time: the many little holes along the side reminded me of the Meccano set that had given me so much joy in my childhood.

Finally, I came to the top. Only then did I notice the little children hanging from the railing of the viaduct like monkeys in their cages at the zoo.

"You better be careful," the biggest among them, a biracial boy, shouted in my direction. "This bridge is under construction, you know."

In spite of his admonition, I slipped as I was climbing along the girder, just managing to hold on with one hand. Focusing all my strength and energy, I pulled myself back up and continued my climb. Exhausted, at last I got to where the children now sat, straddling the railing. Laughing at my struggle, nevertheless, they gave me a hand and deftly pulled me up onto the bridge.

While I desperately tried to catch my breath, the kids shot off a stream of instructions. Their incessant nagging reminded me of my fencing coach at Harvard: good old Edo Marion—he, too used to mutter an uninterrupted torrent of directions that would distract me, just as I was trying to concentrate on stabbing my opponent with my epée.

"You really have got to be very careful," a little bespectacled girl's voice squeaked gravely. "It is a treacherous crossing."

"The bridge is still being repaired," a tiny boy with curly hair and freckles informed me.

"Make sure you hold onto the left railing," the bigger, black boy yelled as he hung upside down from the guardrail. "The pickets of the right one are held together only by some string."

"Besides, they're really loose," the girl with the glasses added.

In the end, I was thankful for their words of caution, although they certainly made me very apprehensive. Never mind, I thought to myself: I have to get across. I must. I glanced along the bridge only to see it metamorphose into three rows of planks that seemed to narrow faster than the laws of perspective would normally dictate.

I gingerly took a step out onto the boards, keeping to the left as much as possible. After the first few strides, I realized that the children had been entirely correct: the whole contraption was very unsteady, very unsafe. I could not turn back, though; there was nothing to do but plod along as best I could. At times, my weight pushed the planks underwater, so that my feet were submerged. The current, too, increased in strength as I approached the middle of the wide river.

Much to my dismay, the left-hand railing eventually dissolved into a net made of string. I tried to reel this web in as rapidly as possible to save myself from sinking. I remember looking down at my feet and thinking that I was literally waterskiing along on one of the boards. This was a losing battle though, and I finally found myself totally immersed. It was really hard work merely to keep my head above the surface.

As I struggled in the fast current, close to drowning, a huge motorboat just missed me. Some people partying on a sailboat—actually, I think it was a converted Chinese junk—all dressed in Roaring Twenties attire, laughed and clapped at my predicament while others danced the Charleston in the background.

An exhausting eternity later, just as I was saying an Act of Contrition for all my sins, preparing for the end, as if by a miracle, I arrived in a calm pool under the bridge. Lo and behold, a few yards ahead of me was the shore, the other side of the river. I'd made it!

I climbed up the bank, a walking wet rag, an amphibian emerging onto *terra firma*. To my surprise, I found myself in a little park that reminded me of the Jardin de Luxembourg in Paris in the *sixième*. Marble benches waited here and there among the meticulously planted flowers and groomed gravel footpaths. Gas lights rose like artificial trees from the cobblestoned ground; at night, they would shed romantic light on anonymous shadows hugging and kissing on the benches or strolling along the walkways.

Now, in the greyness of late afternoon, I noticed that the benches were occupied by a bevy of resting Ethiopians—I guessed, based on their dark, fine features—dressed in the torn rags of slaves. Their wrists and ankles were shackled, and heavy iron balls were attached to the chains on their legs, presumably to prevent them from running away.

"Now dat you've crossed de rivah, ya've da take our shains orf," the biggest of them, perched on the back of one off the benches addressed me menacingly in a patois I had difficulty understanding.

I tried to avoid a potentially unpleasant encounter by sneaking away: my teachers had always told me not to get involved. Through a medieval archway, I passed into a dark and sinister courtyard. I felt miserable, and the fear, on top of the cold and wet, made me shiver uncontrollably. I remember forcing my moist hands into my already full pockets and hunching my back like a cripple—as close as I could get to the fetal position, while still hoping to make some progress.

I hurried across the courtyard. Right in the middle of it, a man with a broad face and a brush cut passed me on a dilapidated bicycle. He was wearing a filthy T-shirt and khaki army pants, and held a fedora that he proceeded to poise atop his head. I don't know why, but I immediately suspected him of being a secret agent. This must have been his first time cycling, though, as he almost knocked me over—his course wavered to and fro like a bull's pizzle when it urinates (to quote an expression my dear father would have used). Much to my delight, the secret agent ran into a brick wall, and while he was down on the ground inspecting his wounds, I managed to escape through another medieval arch.

I entered a sunny little park, much like the one where the Ethiopians had been lounging around. This one, though, was empty of all life except, much to my chagrin, the secret agent, who dismounted just ahead of me, presumably to allow me to catch up and pass him. He pulled the brim of his hat low over his eyes and, trying to act nonchalant, lit a cigarette. The spooky man loitered in the gardens, whistling gaily and smoking away, ignoring me and pretending to study the colorful petunias.

About midway through this park, the gravel path took a sharp turn to the left. The walk then abruptly arrived at a wall, which it then trailed up a slight incline for some distance. I knew that just beyond the stone barrier ran a major roadway, so I rapidly hoisted myself up and jumped down the other side, hoping that the secret agent would not notice. I landed softly on the sidewalk, straightened my attire, and strolled along as inconspicuously as possible. I was extremely worried though, because I didn't have any identification on me. I knew that in this Communist state, one was not supposed to go anywhere without one's papers, and here I was crossing piazzas, rivers, parks and courtyards, and climbing hills and leaping walls with no documentation whatsoever. Surely a crime of major proportions.

At long last, the roadway came to the intersection of Incline Street, which gradually climbed up Eagle Hill, where I lived. I congratulated myself on having lost my tail, and was about to turn left into Incline Street, when from behind me I heard what I instinctively knew to be the voice of the creepy secret agent ask, "May I come with you, please? I've always had a hankering to go up to the very top!"

I was totally deflated. In a rapid round of mental acrobatics, I came to the conclusion that I was in no position to decline—after all, a street is public property. So, I just ignored the weird operative, and doggedly started up the slope, staying to the right. Over my left shoulder, out of the corner of my eye, I could see the man struggling to keep up, and I took some pleasure in remarking that I was in much better shape. Secretly, I assessed the landscape to my right and noted that there was a cemetery, separated from the road by a ditch and a low wall of loose stones collected from the field

All of a sudden, the man's little dog—a Pekinese, or something equally hideous—that, up until then, I had not noticed, jumped down from his arms where it must have been cuddling and darted playfully into the graveyard where I knew some of my forebears were buried. Annoyed, the man ran across the ditch, hopped over the barrier, and took off after his pet. As the two played hide and go seek among the tombstones, I could hear him shout, "Come here, you little devil!" with frustration in his voice. The pooch yelped like mad, taunting its master to give chase.

Good, I thought, this could be my chance. I dropped into the ditch and crawled like a lizard through weeds and debris in order to try and lose my stalker. I prayed that the secret agent, together with his stupid little rat of a dog, would join the occupants of the graves. After a decent interval, I carefully peeked over the wall. In that very instant, just a few yards ahead of me, out jumped my nemesis, up onto the rocks, laughing and holding the canine demon in one hand while patting his protruding gut with the other.

Angry and feeling guilty at having been caught again, I vigorously continued my jaunt up Incline Street. No longer caring about the inane intelligence operative, I finally reached the house among the trees. I opened the door and walked in, happy to be home. In the salon, empty faces looked at me anxiously and a voice asked, "Where have you been all this time?"

"We were worried about you!" another chided me lovingly.

I did not want to explain, at least not just then, so without further ado, I said, "I'm very tired. I'd like to go to bed."

Someone showed me to my room, one of the attic cubicles. There was no bed there, just a rocking chair facing the door and a book lying open on the floor. Curious, I picked up the volume, sat in the rocker, and started reading it from back to front. I read and read and read for hours; the novel—for it was fiction and very well written—was impossible to put down.

After an enthralling eternity, I heard footsteps slowly ascending the stairs. As I was decidedly not feeling sociable—I did not want to be interrupted in the middle of reading, and because the day's events had truly exhausted me—I feigned sleep. The steps finally reached the top, the door creaked open, and through the slits in my eyes, I saw an arm reach into the room from the darkness of the stairwell and vehemently shove an object right to my feet.

I listened apprehensively as the intruder, hopefully not that wicked secret agent delivering an explosive, descended again. I finally dared to open my eyes wide, jumped up to close the door, and picked up the strange packet. Closer examination revealed that it was a box wrapped in blue and green paper and neatly tied with a pink ribbon. A present! Avidly, I tore the parcel open, only to find my old exam books. The marks, as I flipped through them, were quite good: thirty-five out of forty-one, a hundred and eleven out of a hundred and seventeen, nineteen out of twenty-three, and so on.

Twice I searched through the pile, but I was aghast that one exam was clearly missing. Yes, the history one. I anxiously tried to remember where it might be. Perhaps I had never turned it in when I finished. Oh, no, that would mean I'd failed history!

To my great relief, in the next instant, I remembered that the missing exam book had been returned to me with a passing mark clearly displayed on it shortly after I sat for the test; I just had not handed it back, as was required. So I must have had it all this time or lost it somewhere in the flow of my life. Not to worry; it didn't matter much now.

Nevertheless, my old exams filled me with pride. But I could not dwell on them too long for the telephone rang incessantly. I finally succumbed to the urgent seeming call and reached out from under the covers to answer.

It was my brother, Peter. He was calling to announce that his wife, Sue, had just borne him a daughter.

I was an uncle.

The Birthday Party

I

The taxi driver pulled up in front of Marcia's building and honked three times, exactly as I'd instructed. Within seconds, my girlfriend appeared in the doorway and I was struck once again by how lucky I was to have such a beautiful partner.

This time, fortunately, she was ready. Highly uncharacteristic of the woman I loved. Usually, I would be fidgeting nervously and like someone deranged, talking to myself, asking what could she be doing in there while the meter ticked away. Maybe on this occasion she'd taken on board my insistence that arriving on time to this party was supremely important.

Marcia paused another precious moment to lock her front door, then skipped down the steps and climbed in beside me. Breathless, she pecked a kiss on my lips as she struggled to close the door, and finally, the taxi was on its way.

After complimenting Marcia on her punctuality (did I sound a bit too sarcastic?), with a smug smile, I started to unzip the vinyl sports bag I'd been hugging protectively under my right arm. This was one of my prize possessions, part of the equipment given every member of the Canadian Olympic team. What particularly endeared this kitbag to me were the five interwoven Olympic rings and the words *Montreal 1976* emblazoned on its red sides, proudly proclaiming that its owner had participated in the Games. To show Marcia, I enthusiastically pulled the two magnum bottles of ruby red Bellefleur wine I had bought for the party. And, more gingerly, the smaller bottle of Chateau Margaux

1970, for the birthday girl. Although I really hoped she would share this wonderful Bordeaux with us.

"Oh, we'll be sure to have enough wine," Marcia remarked with the little smile I loved. "I also brought a bottle," she added, extracting a twenty-six ouncer from a brown paper bag.

"Never mind. I'm sure that the two of us will be able to consume the two magnums as well as your bottle," I said, to tease her. "I suspect that this party will be a long and drawn-out affair." And I pulled her closer to me.

"Perhaps we should share with some of the others, don't you think?" Marcia asked rhetorically, as we started necking.

"Well, maybe," I muttered between kisses. "I guess I want to be in form for later."

While we were still absorbed in each other in the back seat, the driver pulled up to the curb on a tree-lined avenue, opposite what—when I looked up from Marcia's closed eyes—I recognized to be the right house. We had arrived in front of a smallish bungalow with a well-kept front garden and a stone walkway leading to the front door. A huge black head with curly hair, bulging, blood-shot eyes and smiling lips, turned around to say the obvious, "Well, here you are, dude!"

"How much do we owe you?" I asked the face.

Marcia automatically pulled out an immense wad of loose bills from her always-messy purse and handed the driver a twenty.

"Keep the change," my lover instructed the back of the head as she opened the door of the cab.

It was not until I was about to slam the taxi's door that I spotted the loose pile of bills scattered on the seat Marcia had just vacated. I jumped back in to retrieve the small fortune my girlfriend had absentmindedly almost lost. After this traumatic experience, I held her elbow with my free hand to cross the road, and gently chided her for her carelessness. "Boy, that was close. We almost lost all that you had."

She was almost in tears, so I gave her a kiss. "Never mind. It's only money."

Still, not a good start for the party, I thought, as we ascended the steps.

II

I nervously rang the bell. I never liked the awkward first few moments entering a bash already in full swing. The tremendous din from inside was filtered by the huge wooden door, and through the three small amber windows set in the oak slab, we could see distorted ghostly figures floating around. Finally, the nameless birthday girl came to the door in a satin salmon dress and ushered us through the jaws of the party amidst the usual phony "Oh, how glad to see you" greetings.

My father was there, lounging in the anteroom, spiffy in his tails and white tie, hair meticulously in place, sipping champagne. I leaned down to impart the tender brush on the cheek customary between European males and kissed my mother who stood beside him, gorgeous in a navy-blue ball gown, and beamed the special smile of pride mothers reserve for their sons.

The party sucked me, like a powerful magnet, into its very bowels. A residual force towed Marcia and my parents faithfully in my wake. It was as if we were on a slow conveyor belt rolling toward the heart of darkness. Or rather being rolled, for I felt that my role was entirely passive, that it was not my will but some superior law of coincidence generating the string of events.

Without interrupting our gradual progress, I greeted a group of seated guests, all in long evening dresses and dinner jackets or tails—my parents' friends, some relatives, a few people I didn't know. Aunt Lily jumped up in joy, presumably at seeing me, and rushed over to plant a kiss on my cheek. Senile Uncle Béla dropped a caustic comment under his breath—something like, "Oh, here they are, finally, stealing the show!" as he adjusted his pince-nez to ogle Marcia's well-formed breasts. I was particularly glad to see my paternal grandmother seated regally in a burgundy velvet upholstered armchair over in the corner, so I went over to demonstrate the requisite gentle deference and bowed to kiss her on the forehead. Marcia greeted her in a similar fashion, but with slightly more remove.

Behind the seated group of chatting guests, through some open French doors, in the smoke of the next room, I could see Vadiñho in his rumpled white suit, his well-greased black hair slicked back, sitting at the blackjack table twirling the tip of his mustache between thumb and forefinger, about to ask for his third card. For the sake of Cartesian completeness—although I was positive that only I would hear above the din—I shouted, "*Olà*, Vadiñho!" and then, "Good luck." He turned his head slightly toward me, smiled and winked, as if to acknowledge my greeting.

On my right, I noticed some big open double glass doors through which I passed to the patio and garden, still followed by Marcia and my parents. The conveyor belt carried us past the myriad of faceless guests, over toward the left, where I knew instinctively the tennis courts were. The very moment we reached these, my attention was captured by the victory bellow of a wavy-haired boy who had just vanquished his wavy-but-grey-haired father, whom he resembled so closely, that I suspected the son was a clone. The father obviously resented losing to his son, for he had trouble masking his sour scowl. He walked off the court in a huff without bothering to congratulate his offspring.

I looked away from this unpleasant domestic scene, only to spy my friend Mal back in the rear right corner of the garden. I hurried over to say hello, hoping, as I went, that together we would be able to concoct some boyish prank or engage in a wild adventure. When I observed that Mal was wearing his schoolboy shorts, I knew we were sure to have some fun.

"Let's blow this pop stand." Mal was bored and wanted to leave. He had no trouble in enticing me to squeeze through the garden's rear hedge, formed by cedar clones, to where the vast, timeless parkland sloped down toward the sea.

III

It was a beautiful day, so Mal and I gaily set out in our shorts and sneakers through the trees, down toward the beach, at times running, at times walking, slapping each other on the back, and telling lewd jokes and grossly exaggerated tales of our exploits. Our happy banter was interrupted by S. Morgan crossing our path—he almost knocked us over with the supreme effort he was still expending as he tried to win the high school cross-country race. His tortured face and hairless chest were drenched in sweat. Despite this disturbance, we made good time and within a short while, came to an area sparsely covered with low shrubs where the soil turned sandy. Here, we started sprinting down the concave beach toward the azure blue water.

All of a sudden, it dawned on me that the entire time, our subconscious destination had been exactly this point along the beach, for this was where the beautiful, gentle nymph—the one who dressed in orange rags, whom we'd all been in love with as children—lived. Her home was a bright blue plastic pup tent erected on a float moored to a stake with a long, somewhat tattered rope. We considered ourselves lucky: our girl was there, in front of the tent and as pleased as ever to see us. She said she often thought of us—her musketeers, as she liked to call us—and she'd missed us very much since our last visit. I was still in love with her from my preteen days (don't tell Marcia!). Her bewitching smile was the sun, shining at me from among those blonde tresses. Her eyes, I knew, were the sea.

Our nymph left her bobbing float to join us on shore and we all sat down on the beach right where the tiny, cooling waves met the warm sand. I could not help staring at her, but the radiance she exuded was overwhelming, too much for me. Absentmindedly, I dug around in the sand and picked up an open clam shell deserted by its occupant. When I touched it though, it broke in two. Guiltily, I looked at our nymph—for she was the goddess of nature—but she only laughed, a beautiful, slow-motion sun flare, and pointed to the dozens of clams crowding around her raft, proud to be the guards specially chosen to protect her from marauders who might approach her nest from the water.

We were very happy sitting there by the sea, we three. We didn't exchange any words; there was no need to, for we shared all our feelings, all our thoughts, instantaneously, as if we were one being. The gentle lapping of the waves was only broken by the occasional cascading laugh when one of us would erupt, no longer able to contain the ecstasy within. Eons passed, or seconds; time was inconsequential.

But like all idylls, ours too, had to end. Our euphoria was interrupted when I noticed someone running toward us and shouting, all in a frenzy, "Look out! Run!"

Mal and the nymph too, raised their eyes from the sand, and when our rather puzzled brains finally analyzed the prospect we were gazing out upon, we observed that a woman from the ancient Piltdown tribe—in my rapture, I had forgotten that this ancient clan lived near here—was frantically sprinting toward us and gesticulating toward the open sea. Our peepers followed her pointing fingers and sure enough, closing rapidly in on us, skimming over the water like a hovercraft, were the protruding neck and ugly head of one of those monstrous, turtle-like reptiles I remembered from the J for Jurassic section of my childhood encyclopedia. Its forked tongue popped out of its huge beak in cycles alternating with the rhythmic pulsations of its immense, venous eyes. And these were focused on us and nothing else.

We—more precisely, I—panicked, and wildly started to clamber up the concave wall of the beach. Our girl in orange, wonderful person that she was, stopped for a moment to wait for the beautiful, but not quite human seeming, Piltdown woman, who was risking her life to warn us of the approach of the terrible monster. That instant of hesitation was just enough for the beast to catch her at the same time it reached the Piltdown girl. Mal and I peered out from our hiding place among the shrubs and to our horror, we could see it, the turtle-monster, now all warty head, liquid eyes and scaly arms, a repugnant reptilian reincarnation of

Humpty Dumpty, manhandling our beloved nymph and about to sink its huge incisors into the Piltdown woman's jugular.

The ladies fought and squirmed and screamed. Our nymph clambered onto the monster's neck, and with her delicate arms framed one of its bulging blood-shot eyes, into which both she and the Piltdown lass desperately tried to stick gobs of fat leeches they had managed to gather in their palms. In my frustration, I looked around for a stick, a piece of driftwood, a rock, any projectile to heave at the beast, but couldn't find anything. Mal, ever cool and calm, reached behind the bushes and pulled out an elephant gun.

Just what was needed, I thought.

"Please, for god's sake, be careful," I pleaded, "whatever you do, don't hit one of the girls." As he took aim, I added, "You know the Piltdown people don't dare attack this species of turtle. They're normally much too afraid. Why, it's even dangerous for big-game hunters to take on the turtle-monster."

The shot rang out. In the unearthly growling and screaming that followed, Mal and I managed instantaneously to make it up to an outcrop overlooking the panorama of the beach and the sea. Over to the left, in the mouth of an unnamed river, we could see an armada of the slender Piltdown boats rushing to rescue their girl and our beloved nymph.

"It really is too bad, Mal," I remarked, "that these excellent people became extinct during the Stone Age. Evolution sometimes yields strange results, doesn't it?"

IV

Saddened by those terrible events on the beach—which, with each step, slipped further into the realm of amnesia—we sauntered aimlessly through the trees. Our unconscious path led toward the top of the rise and was only interrupted by J. Simpson, naked save for his horn-rimmed glasses, dragging a huge cross through the woods, much like Christ on the way to Golgotha.

After what seemed to be an eternal climb, we finally reached the summit. We crossed through that miraculous hedge again and found ourselves back in the garden teeming with the partying guests. "What have we missed?" we asked a faceless, bare-chested merrymaker holding a drink precariously in one hand. "What's happening?"

"Well, most of the guests are playing parlor games. But if you're interested, there is a fantastic show in the big gymnasium. Over there, behind the tennis courts," the shirtless wonder waved his arm without pointing in any decipherable direction.

Mal and I galloped enthusiastically to where I knew the gymnasium was. Inside, on the dimly lit parquet floor, the performance was already in full progress. Four columns of soldiers wearing bright red hussar uniforms hung with golden braids and tall, tasseled hats marched up and down the length of the basketball court. Back and forth, like a pendulum. As they approached the walls at either end, they lifted their arms and legs higher and higher, until right before they did an about-turn, they were doing the goose step. Much to my dismay, I saw them raise their arms in the *Heil Hitler!* salute. They were like puppets on strings, soldiers manipulated by an external force.

As my eyes gradually adjusted to the darkness, I started to make out all the partygoers, including my parents and Marcia, sitting around the edge of the gymnasium in their long dresses and dinner jackets on folding metal seats expressly brought there for this show. I blew my girlfriend a kiss and waved to my parents. I also noticed that only two of the numerous big fans placed in the small alcoves around the gym were working. I resolved to take this matter up later with the management.

Without any warning or announcement, the soldiers marched out, all except one column. These men were then joined by three rows of hussar cavalry in red uniforms, drawn sabers glittering in the lights, riding prancing and wheezing horses. One column lined up on one side of the remaining string of foot soldiers while the other two positioned themselves on the other side. The four rows now started to perform the very same inane maneuvers that the foot soldiers had presented earlier. The hussars on their horses—which were also doing the goose step, so much so, that they literally took off from the ground—would almost touch the high ceiling with the tips of their swords as they reached the wall at either end.

During these quasi-military antics, I leaned against the doorway hoping something exciting would happen. When it became evident that the show consisted of nothing but this boring, repetitive to and fro marching, we left, disillusioned, cursing the faceless guest who had advised us to come over to the gymnasium to see it.

V

I wandered through several rooms until I came to a grey chamber with a patch of grey linoleum at the center, free of guests. In the middle of this circle, I saw some papers, which, on closer examination looked like a copy of an article, slightly frayed or singed at the edges. The merrymakers gaily partying in this room consciously ignored the grey patch and the article, except for the occasional nervous glance. I squatted down to read the excerpt and ascertained that it was from a recent *Time* magazine reporting on the self-immolation of journalist Walter Schramm. His suicide note claimed he burned himself out of disgust at the demise of Western Civilization, and more particularly, to protest the depravity and weakness of the US presidency. This stupidity and lack of backbone, more than anything else, according to Schramm, was why we were presently experiencing a return to the Dark Ages.

Shramm's self-sacrifice and thesis were rather intriguing, so I set out to find my friend J. Simpson, who had been editor-in-chief of our high school yearbook. Perhaps he could shed more light on Schramm's views and suicide. I ambled back toward the gymnasium and turned into a side chamber on the hunch that he, too, would be watching the boring performance back there after our earlier encounter among the trees. This side chamber was obviously just in the process of being renovated, for all its walls, as well as the ceiling and floor were lined with plywood.

I finally ran into Simpson in the doorway of one of the dressing rooms adjoining the gymnasium. My friend was now dressed up in tails and top hat like the other partygoers and no longer carried the heavy crucifix on his shoulders.

"What do you think of Walter Schramm's suicide?" I confronted him with the question that had been bothering me.

"Yes, I heard about it just the other day." He readjusted his glasses on his nose. "It really is too bad, you know. He was being touted as a possible candidate in the upcoming presidential election."

"You're right. It really is a pity." I nodded my agreement, as my eyes glanced across the plywood-covered room, over to where my friends—George Spyrou, Norman Beatty and others—were horsing around in the elevator. They must have been stoned, I thought, because they were giggling and pressing all the buttons at the same time. From the darkness on the other side of the doorway, R. Boxer greeted me fleetingly. Behind him, I spied Mal approaching, still in his schoolboy shorts, so I left J. Simpson and joined my friend from Expo 70.

"You know, it's time to go to the showers," Mal informed me, "since this stupid show is finally over."

Just then, the doors of the gymnasium opened, and we were swept away by a tide of women in long dresses and big flowery hats, carrying parasols, accompanied by gentlemen in tails or dinner jackets. The crowd carried us through many rooms full of similarly attired guests partying and playing parlor games. I looked desperately for Marcia and my parents, but they were nowhere to be seen.

Finally, at the far end of the mansion, we tumbled into a ballroom where cloned children discoed to the strains of *Saturday Night Fever* and the command of "one two three, one two three," shouted over and over again by a stern dance master armed with a whip that he cracked in time to the music. He was dressed for the circus in a lion trainer's uniform, sky-blue, trimmed with golden braids. The swell of the crowd was just barely strong enough to carry us past a bar, which we realized was probably the last one before the showers, so we looped back around for a drink.

"We don't serve exotic cocktails here," the mustachioed barman answered. "We only serve straight alcohol, since this is a bar for children."

We turned away, annoyed that we would not be served. As we attempted to pass through the next doorframe, a filthy little old man sitting by a folding card table yelled at us in a squeaky voice, "Hey, buddy, you ain't allowed to take those games away from the restricted area. Under no circumstances . . ."

It was only then that I realized that I had a whole series of bits of different games under my right arm. One by one, I placed them on the tabletop in front of the codger: half a chess board, half a backgammon board, and half a *Monopoly* board, all bottoms up, along with two very used ping pong rackets. Mal picked these all up again, to check that indeed they were games and not something else, and once satisfied, put them back in a pile, right side up. I managed to sneak past the old guard with the empty *Monopoly* box under my arm.

Mal had learned that the showers were down the corridor to the left, through an entrance marked with drooping red letters. Once we reached the door, I pushed it open and saw that the tiled room was completely empty. From the wall opposite protruded three singularly ugly showerheads, and a somewhat less hideous one hung from the end wall. Still carrying the monopoly box, I beelined for the single showerhead, even though it was quite a bit farther, avoiding the dripping outlets that graced the other wall. Somehow, I suspected it would be the best one. Not only was it the most attractive of the four, but I was sure it would be the only one that might produce hot water. I turned the faucet to test my hunch, and sure enough, the water that came out in a jet was steaming hot. In the process, though, the *Monopoly* box became soggy, so in a fit of rage, I threw it into the hall along with my drenched clothes.

I showered, relishing the gentle, but warm pricks of the

tumbling droplets. After a few moments, the door opened, and a shorthaired girl with glasses walked in.

"Excuse me," she said somewhat apologetically, "but I'm wondering if I could use one of the showers here. The ladies' don't work."

"Sure, by all means," I retorted, eager to please.

Satisfied, the woman left. Next a man entered, and without a word, proceeded to try some of the other outlets. With a frown, he gave up, came over to me and asked, "Could I use that shower when you're finished? That's the one with the most pressure in the hot water pipes."

I wasn't especially in a hurry, so I took my time without answering. The man waited, fidgeting. Then two girls I judged to be in their late teens, with short dark hair and lanky legs, walked in, still dressed in running shorts, T-shirts and spikes.

"Did you ladies make the Italian team?" the man who was waiting for the shower asked, meaning, obviously, the Italian track team.

"No," the taller girl answered, "because Canada is always discriminated against. For example," she continued, pulling her top over her head, "television announcers can't even pronounce *Canada* properly. Instead, they say, 'Canadia'."

I could not help but stare at her beautiful breasts, and I became aroused as she stripped off her remaining clothes.

VI

The reference to the -a/-ia conundrum brought me back to the office in a flash: Bill Kilfoyle, my boss at the Inter-American Development Bank, and I were discussing the propensity for confusing the two.

"You know, Geza, I would really like to get to the bottom of this issue," he said. "Why don't you ask the controllers for a study on which countries in the Bank have names ending in -ia or -ina."

Bill was visibly excited: he thought he was really on to something big. Gingerly, because I did not have the heart to deflate his enthusiasm, I answered, "It should be quite easy to find out the facts. Even Fiona, my secretary, or I should be able to do the study in just a few minutes by looking at the list of governors of the Bank and the countries they represent."

And with my return to the office, the external reality of routine existence had created a breach. The birthday party was long since over, and I opened my eyes. Only the ephemeral sensation of having been at the anniversary bash remained, hung there for a fleeting moment, until it too, evaporated in the sunlight.

The King of Knaves

"All right, sweetie," Marcia announced glibly, "I'm off now." My beautiful girlfriend was wrapped in her waist-length mink jacket over an above-the-knee dress and high heels. She could easily have passed for a fashion model out of *Vogue*. Framed in the doorway of the lavatory, she beamed a smile that reminded me of Leonardo's *Mona Lisa*.

Mona Marcia, I thought, as I was very happy at that moment sitting there on the throne.

"Ooookay." I grunted impatiently as I got up from the toilet bowl. I had been completely engrossed in trying to master an oversized piece of fecal matter and I didn't want Marcia's departure to interrupt my concern as to whether it would make it down the somewhat frail plumbing in our ramshackle house.

"I'll see you later," I mumbled. But my mind was following the voyage into the netherworld of my stool.

Or had it by now turned into a rat? I wondered with an internal smile.

"I'm going up the Knoll," Marcia said. "Would you be so kind as to bring my Around-the-World makeup kit with you when you finish . . . whatever you are doing there? And do get off the pot now. I can't for the life of me see the attraction of sitting there for so long. Your father always said you would get hemorrhoids from straining too hard, remember? So, get off!"

* * *

I left the house on the edge of the copse at the bottom of the hill just a few minutes after Marcia. The narrow path that began at the backdoor threaded through the trees and angled over toward the dirt road leading up the steep slope behind the property. This was the Knoll of Knaves, as the locals called it. On either side of the track, the vegetation was lush and green. Huge fronds beat against my calfskin boots as I tried to keep the stabbing branches away from my face with my hands and elbows.

It was only a few hundred yards to the road, but by the time I reached it, I was perspiring profusely. That was another difference between Marcia and me: I loved to sweat, whereas she found it disgusting and only tolerated it when we made love. As I clambered out of the ditch onto the dirt road, I noticed that about twenty yards ahead, still on the side the house was situated on, a deserted yellow cab was pulled over, pointing uphill. A very anxious policeman, hat tipped back and pencil and pad poised to issue a ticket, was pleading with the lifeless machine.

"You shouldn't be here! You shouldn't be here," the young officer, almost in tears, repeated over and over again like a scratched record.

I could not allow my attention to linger on this seemingly innocuous but inane activity, as another thirty or forty yards along the roadway, in the open entranceway of a rickety garage constructed from rotting planks, two other policemen were trying to disarm and arrest a dark-haired, somber, sallow faced young man in a bright red flannel shirt. The youth, who from afar could be mistaken for a Native American, wielded a sleek Kalashnikov. He had a scared, hunted look on his face, but from where I was, it was difficult to tell whether he or the police were more afraid.

I quickly assessed the situation to be extremely perilous: I would be risking life and limb were I to pass in front of the garage. One could never foretell what such dangerous psychotics might do from one moment to the next, nor where stray bullets might lodge during a shootout. I did not want to be the dead victim of a stupid accident, so I hightailed it away from there as fast as possible.

On the other side of the lane was a pile of huge basalt boulders. I scurried across to hide behind them until the crisis up the slope diffused. Just as I pulled myself behind the safety of the mound, the young man, still waving threateningly with his machinegun, broke away from the policemen and ran across to my side of the street. The officers scrambled after him. I was trembling. I knew it was now or never, if I wanted to stay alive: my only chance was to run for the other side and attempt to regain the safety of the house.

Fleeing along the path, I congratulated myself for having escaped from the danger posed by the youth. However, when I arrived home, I remembered that Marcia was still waiting for her Around-the-World makeup kit up on top of the Knoll of Knaves. She was no doubt wondering whether I'd managed to get off the toilet. (*Or perhaps whether the rat and its friends had gotten me?*)

And, of course, while she was waiting on the summit, she, too, was in peril from the likes of the man in the red flannel shirt. Nevertheless, she simply could not go to work without putting on her makeup—at least that's what she claimed, because for my part, I thought she was beautiful without it.

I sat down in my favorite beige corduroy armchair in the living room to wade through these disturbing thoughts. Finally, I convinced myself that the danger posed by the young man had probably passed and it would be safe for me to make another attempt to climb the Knoll of Knaves.

* * *

In no time at all, I was back on the dirt road. I jogged past the garage where the standoff had taken place earlier, but fear prevented me from yielding to the temptation of looking through the gaping, dark doorway of the shack. When I finally reached the plateau, I realized that it was not the need to deliver Marcia's Around-the-World makeup that had brought me to the summit, but rather some other force that was shaping my destiny. This power, this iron will, had taken hold of me, directed me: and now told my defenseless subconscious that it was the path to the left, the one leading to the edge of the cliff that I had to take.

Without breaking my gait, I veered slightly to the left. This track was even more overgrown than the one that led from the house to the dirt road. There were moments that seemed like eons, when I scarcely made any progress. Reaching the precipice, my advance was further impeded by chicken wire enmeshed in the undergrowth, presumably to prevent people from falling over. At times now, I was crawling through folds of chicken wire, at times, it was the interwoven chain and the undergrowth that kept me from plummeting thousands of feet to the valley below. I was literally squeezing myself along the wire fence, perilously poised above the abyss. It was tough going, to say the least, and the sense of foreboding and fear never left me.

Finally, after many hours of excruciating work, I reached a small clearing at the edge of the cliff—that is, rather a patch clear of undergrowth but still with a canopy of branches that formed a roof and turned the little open area into a cave. It was here, I instinctively knew, that my rendezvous with the King of Knaves would take place.

* * *

I crawled out of sight, just over the edge of the precipice, so that I was swinging in mid-air, held up by the chicken wire and the overflowing undergrowth with the gorge far below. After a wait that seemed interminable and during which I must have dozed off, from the other end of the tree-cave, where a patch of blue sky showed through, suddenly some commotion activated my already abnormally acute senses. I longed for it to be the King and his entourage. But just as I was about to peak over the edge, a shadow loomed over me. The dark-haired young man in the red flannel shirt leaned over the side with a mean smile on his face and menacingly fingered the trigger of his machinegun.

I knew in a flash that I had to act quickly, or I would suffer a gruesome death. Mustering a superhuman effort, I lunged upwards and grabbed his right leg, taking him by surprise, and pulled the crook over the edge. He fell to the valley floor thousands of feet below, screaming, "I didn't do it! I didn't do it!" I had no idea what deed he meant.

In that same instant, I saw another evil-looking man, balding and in a denim shirt and dirty, torn jeans arrive, with his pistol cocked and ready to shoot. Even though the previous effort had totally sapped my strength, when he came to the precipice to look for me, I leaped up and grabbed the bald man's left leg, plunging him to a certain and bloody death in the abyss below. I didn't dare follow the falling body with my eyes for fear of vertigo.

Now completely spent, I was barely able to hang on in my nest of chicken wire. Fortunately, the two policemen arrived a few minutes later, panting for breath. They dragged me up onto solid ground just as I was about to let go from sheer fatigue. I remember thinking that I felt as limp as Christ must have after he was taken down from the cross. But I was not ready to be buried yet, even if Resurrection might have been in store.

"Gee, you were terrific!" the stockier of the policemen complimented me. "You helped rid society of a real public menace. In fact, not one, but two."

"Come! Let's go for a drink." The smaller, but older, mustachioed officer tried to pull me up from where I had flopped. "You certainly deserve one."

When they saw that I had trouble climbing out of my lair, they pulled me up and lifted me to their shoulders to carry me to help them celebrate this momentous victory of good over evil.

"Naw, I am sorry. I can't go with you," I declined dutifully. "I have to wait for the others."

The policemen finally left me to myself. Just as I was about to settle on a rotting tree trunk to rest my shattered self, my entire family—parents, brothers, sisters—popped out of the forest and greeted me noisily.

"Hey! Let's play *Scrabble*." My youngest sister Susan waved the board of her favorite game above her head. "I'm going to be the winner!" She pronounced *winner* as if it were *wiener*.

We set up the *Scrabble* board on the edge of the cliff and circled around it like a baboon troop contemplating its evening meal. I was seated on a wooden barstool so tall its legs were planted securely somewhere in the valley below. To reach the *Scrabble* board, I had to stretch across empty space, a veritable void. The rest of the family sat around in the moss on the edge of the cliff and we played merrily, with lots of shouting and frequent accusations of cheating. While I was waiting for my father to take his turn—he always took an inordinately long time—I realized that perching on the stool probably wasn't such a good idea. After all, the demon of the dark young man in the red flannel shirt, or that of his balding ally, might at any moment resurrect and topple the stool.

"Peter, help me climb onto firmer ground," I implored my brother. Clinging to him, I pushed the stool away with my feet. Without much effort on my part, it tipped over and, I hoped, crushed the spirits of those terrible criminals if they were still active in the valley below. From then on, I wasn't able to focus on the *Scrabble*; my senses were keenly tuned, listening for the imminent arrival of the King of Knaves and his entourage.

Sure enough, a loud fanfare announced their approach. The entire crew filed, with great pomp and circumstance, into the cave formed by the vegetation. All the participants in the solemn possession wore fancy robes or full-length dresses that reminded me of the costumes we used in *the* play within the play in our high school productions of *Hamlet*. Their faces were somewhat unreal and distorted, but not in an unpleasant way, and painted apple green and off-white. I found these visitors somewhat reminiscent of rag dolls, yet they were delightfully alive and almost human. The king and the princess sported real crowns of gold like the ones in the fairytales of my childhood, with small golden orbs on the ends of each prong. Their movements, the actions of these pseudo-people, were measured and languid. Seeing them march at a leisurely pace into the clearing was like watching a slow-motion movie.

The king and his followers were extremely polite and pleasant. One by one, they introduced themselves to my family, who were very taken by these fairytale aristocrats. My father and the king bowed to each other, much like Japanese businessmen. The king, in his booming voice, apologized to me for having arrived late. And the princess, whom I knew from a previous surreptitious rendezvous, took my arm and swept me over to where five or six members of the entourage were sitting on a fallen tree trunk. She snuggled up to me and pointed at this happy group, saying, "These are the metallic boys. They are really good people to know. In case you are ever in trouble."

With that, she led me to the entrance of the tree cave at the side farthest from the precipice, the entrance through which they, and my family too, had all arrived. Arms linked, we stepped out into the blinding sun and looked over the balustrade along the edge, down onto a totally new part of the valley. Pointing to the dizzying reaches below (as I took great delight in her firm breasts against me), my princess friend proudly exclaimed, "Look, look! See how successful the metallic boys are at evacuating the city."

And as my gaze followed the pointing of her beautiful, slender arm and index finger, I saw miniscule people streaming out of the side of the mountain, like worms from wet earth after a summer rainstorm. It was a scene from a biblical film: the backs of veiled and hooded forms blindly following an imaginary savior.

"They are preparing the city for you." I felt the princess's sweet-smelling warm breath brush my ear. "For my father intends to make you king."

I looked into her deep blue eyes and kissed her, wondering what my future as King of the Knaves held in store for me.

Alas, I would never know. The very next moment, I woke from the dream.

Vacation

My roving eyes flew over bobbing heads, those of the several members of my family seated across the table from me. My peepers continued their tour through the large, tinted windows of the opulently furnished restaurant in our hotel. Once outside, on the other side of the patio, they rested for a second on the palm-lined stone walk that led down to the glistening beach. Then the twins picked up the pace as they staggered along the path, hesitating only momentarily at the undulating boundary of the beach as each wave disappeared into the sand. Then the two skimmed along the trail that continued on perfectly, just as the laws of perspective dictated, clear across the open expanse toward the thin horizontal line where sea met sky. Horizon and imaginary walkway intersected at this substance-less point, like the arms of a crucifix extruded by a spaghetti machine. My eyes, however, did not take kindly to this cross: they now had four options, four lines to consider. Should they separate? But then each eye would still have two choices. Perplexed, they aborted their senseless mission, and flew, like vagabond fleas, back into the restaurant, ending their adventurous flight in the sockets in a head that crowned the neck on top of the body lounging on the seat in the hotel's eatery.

The waiters cleared plates covered with well-chewed bones, lumps of fat, shreds of skin, crumpled napkins, and morsels of food left in front of drowsy clients. Conversation at our table—around which my usually effervescent family was strategically dispersed—too, lagged. Chairs had been pushed back, torsos permitted to slouch, limbs splayed for maximum comfort. Sated stomachs were allowed to assume the distended maximum contours of their skin and clothing casing. The pink straws through which hi-balls or exotic drinks had been drained were folded up or broken, and their ends had been well masticated. I was leaning back, balancing on the chair's rear legs, despite my father's and Marcia's periodic looks of displeasure.

Lunch was unquestionably over.

I knew it was time for us to disperse when Marcia got up as she firmly pushed my hovering left knee down, saying impatiently, "Geza, you're going to fall backwards and hurt yourself. And then that will be it."

To which my father added, "Yes, and you'll break that two-hundred-and-forty-dollar chair, and the hotel will add it to our bill. Just wait and see!"

I rolled my eyes and allowed the chair to drop forward onto its four legs.

The nine grownups in our immediate family, as well as Peter and Sue's several children, had come to this somewhat deserted Caribbean island for our first communal vacation in years. This was our fourth day—or was it our fifth?—so we were already acquainted with the many delights the isle held. We lazily contemplated what might come next: our minds, foggy from food and drink, tried to focus on how to extract the maximum hedonistic pleasure from the remains of the day.

"I think we should all have a siesta." My father was known to prescribe sleep after every meal. At the very least, for himself.

"Peter, you're always tired. No wonder! You get up so early. This hour is already way past your bedtime." My mother spiced her rejoinder with a hint of reproach, as was called for in the recipe of their relationship.

My dad was indeed an early riser; he was often out on the tennis courts at five in the morning with his diminutive friend, whose real name was Ady, but we had dubbed the Penguin since he resembled one. Or if the Antarctic bird happened not to be available, the hulking Cookie Monster, another of his childhood friends—who, by the way, kept a lioness as a pet—would be summoned. Fortunately, my dad never dared wake me for a game at such an ungodly hour.

"Why don't we play tennis?" came Marcia's suggestion from behind my chair, where she had been standing and stroking my hair. Always keen to exercise, she was fit and trim in spite of her legendary appetite. Some of the bad mouths surrounding our family jokingly spread the false rumor that she sported a tapeworm. But I knew better.

"Great idea! Let's do it." I was always a keen tennis partner.

"Well, I guess I can sleep later." When it came right down to it, my father was willing to forgo his afternoon siesta in exchange for a good game of tennis.

"Okay. I'll come too." Susie, my youngest sister volunteered to make up the foursome. Tennis, with the possible exception of canasta (or *Scrabble* in the case of Susan), was the most popular game in our family.

The four of us enthusiastically excused ourselves from the table. I let out a wild "Whoopie!" and ran back into the hotel and along the corridor toward the elevators. The others followed in single file at a more leisurely pace.

The elevators were slow in coming. The one we finally caught seemed to take an eternity to reach our stop, three levels up. When it eventually ground to a halt for the third time, I burst through the opening metallic doors, leaving the others to find their own rooms. We had taken separate lodgings, some on different floors even, to maximize our privacy.

In a good mood, I hopped, skipped and jumped toward my room at the very end. I was pleasantly surprised to note that the walls and the ceiling—as well as, of course, the floor—of the hallway were covered in a thick, maroon broadloom, much like in a padded cell. If I were to fall in my mad haste, at the very least, I wouldn't get hurt too badly, I told myself.

Approaching my room, I noticed that the door was slightly ajar. Perhaps it's the maid, I thought. But there was no trolley with clean towels and sheets and fresh bars of soap, bottles of shampoo and conditioner parked outside in the corridor. Perplexed, I cautiously pushed the door open. A low droning emanated from inside, and keening my ears, I distinguished the voices of a man and a woman arguing.

I was completely unprepared for the stunning, leggy brunette who haughtily stood by my bed, with her maroon overcoat loosely slung over her otherwise bare shoulders, cleavage peering forth from a low-cut chocolate silk camisole underneath, tanned thighs tantalizingly exposed in short cutoffs. She held a pink roller bag in each hand and rested the larger of the suitcases on the bed. Only when my eyes had pored over every nook and cranny of this goddess did I notice the fortyish man with thick, black-rimmed glasses by the window. With his well-combed, parted hair, he bore a close resemblance to Clark Kent of *Superman* fame.

"Excuse me, but this happens to be my room," I said with pro-prietary arrogance.

"We're terribly sorry." The brunette—who could have been a sexy Lois Lane—apologized in a husky voice that melted my choler. "There must have been some mistake."

"Yes, they gave us this room at the front desk," Clark Kent waved the plastic keycard that had presumably allowed them entry to my temporary abode.

While the intruders continued to make excuses, I glanced over the contents of the room to confirm that nothing had been taken. I had been warned by previous visitors to these isles that things just disappeared in mysterious ways. As my eyes roved through the room, I noticed that a huge fencing bag resembling the red and black bag I'd bought at Prieur in Paris many years earlier—except for the fact that the red was actually slightly more orange in hue—had been carelessly slung under the rickety fold-away bridge table that served as my desk. In the meantime, the couple's feeble attempt at an explanation had come to a close; Superman and his lady love picked up their bags—including the foreign fencing bag—and left, bowing as they did so, in the formal Japanese manner. At least the Clark Kent impersonator did not offer me a business card. Somewhat short of temper due to this unexpected delay to my tennis plans, I strutted over to the still open door and slammed it shut. I was quite sure that Marcia, my father and Susan were already out on the courts, so I tore my clothes off and changed into my Wimbledon whites.

When I left, I took great care to lock my door, for I did not wish to risk finding some unwanted guests in my room again— even if they might be Superman and his lover—and proceeded back down the corridor to the elevators. This time though, I only jogged, for I did not want to exhaust myself before the big game. As I moved along, limbs loose, I practiced my stroke by hitting the maroon broadloom on the wall here and there with my brand-new Prince racquet.

Fortunately, the elevator arrived much faster than before, and within moments, I was back in the restaurant, then out the other side. I was glad to see that the dining hall was empty and there were no stragglers from my family lingering, still in consumption mode. On the palm-lined path that led from the patio, I bumped into Karen, a girl I'd met in the snack bar the evening before. She, too, was in tennis attire, and looked rather enticing.

"Going for a game?" I asked the obvious.

"Yes. I'm playing with my doctor." She pushed her long black hair out of her eyes and secured it with an elastic band.

We came to where a smaller path headed off to the right, toward the sand dunes, behind which were the courts I always played on. Karen continued straight down the palm-lined main trail.

"The courts are down this way," I tried to correct her.

"No, no. I'm playing over on the beach courts," she insisted, flashing her eyes one more time at me.

"Oh, yes, I forgot about those. They're asphalt, though, aren't they? I prefer to play on clay because of my rickety knees." As soon as the words left my lips, I realized how snobbish they must have sounded. But by then, our ways had parted, so it didn't really matter.

Beside my bad knees, the reason why I really wanted to go the courts behind the sand dunes was that that was where the tennis pro gave his lessons. I was definitely up for a refresher.

As I jogged up to the courts, somewhat out of breath already, I noticed that the pro—who resembled my tennis hero, Arthur Ashe, in every way, except that he used a Prince racquet—was giving a lesson to a chunky American woman with cellulite on the backs of her exposed thighs. This made me angry, and my ire only increased when I noticed that all the courts were taken and my father, Marcia and Susan were nowhere to be seen.

I was fuming as I made my way back to the hotel after this fiasco of a tennis game that never happened. It might be best to go swimming, I thought. That would at least cool my temper, and perhaps salvage something of this valuable afternoon. Reentering the restaurant, I saw Marcia, Susan and my father, all outfitted in their tennis gear, sitting at the same table where we'd eaten lunch. I told them that the courts were taken and proposed my novel idea. Their response was immediate and overwhelming.

"What a great suggestion!" my father shouted as he stood up, ready to go. "Brilliant."

"Yes, let's all go!" Marcia chimed.

"Okay, we're on," my brother Peter, who'd reappeared out of nowhere, also voiced his enthusiasm.

"I love to go swimming." Susan would not be left out. Indeed, she was the best swimmer among us.

We rushed off to our respective rooms to fetch our bathing suits. When I came back down, my father was already waiting for us in front of the hotel, impatient behind the steering wheel of the grey moving van he was driving around those days. We all— Marcia, Mom, Dad, Peter, Susan and I— piled in amidst the usual howls and chaos, and drove off in the direction of the swimming holes that had made this resort so famous.

My father took the curves like a Grand Prix driver and on several occasions, I was sure we would end up in the ditch. After what seemed like an eternity, we finally approached the dip in the landscape where I thought the swimming holes must be. As we made our way down the asphalt incline to the ugly cement structure containing the changing rooms, my father pointed to a weird object that resembled an enormous dunce cap being towed away and said to my mom, "Look, Lily! There is one of those new storage tanks they mass-produce now. See, they are conical, because that shape has been proven scientifically to be the most energy efficient configuration."

"Oh, good. Let's get one of them for our backyard." My mother sounded keen.

"All right. I'll order one when we get home,." my father graciously agreed.

I never quite understood though what those gizmos were good for, other than being energy efficient.

We vacated the van boisterously and marched to the changing rooms. Lockers lined the steel-grey walls and in the middle, there were benches with vertical wooden frames built onto them that held hooks for clothing. Marcia and I consolidated all our family jewels in one of the lockers.

"What do you think, should I hang my new jacket on one of these pegs?" I solicited her advice as I removed my unsoiled grey-blue, vinyl waist length windbreaker with *Cosmos* written on the back. "I sure wouldn't want to ruin it. Or have it stolen."

"Yes," Marcia agreed, "that's probably a very good idea."

I decided to leave on my blue sweatshirt that had *Which way to Pago Pago?* in large red block letters across the chest, even though the underside of the left sleeve was torn. I was sure it was quite cool outside, and I certainly didn't want to freeze.

Marcia and I went back out into the open holding hands and joined the rest of the family, who were by this time milling around the truck. My father was stretched out across the front seat of the moving van. Apparently, he'd already made the decision to stay behind and sleep. He was simply not willing to forego his siesta. My mother, too, had changed her mind. So it was only Peter, Marcia, Susan and I who trekked back up the asphalt slope toward the swimming holes.

Reaching the top of the paved incline, we finally caught sight of the cave-like openings in the three sheer rock faces, ahead of, and to the right and the left of where we were standing. I had the feeling of being dwarfed by a huge grey gravel quarry.

Cloverleaf-like causeways—similar to those one sees on the high-ways of today except that they were much narrower and had solid cement walls about a foot and a half high—led up to the entrances. We were told that we were supposed to slip and slide—more than likely on our stomachs—down these paths before squeezing through the holes to the other side of the quarry wall, where, we believed, all the apertures emptied into one immense basin with beautiful, refreshing, clean water. And it was there that we were supposed to swim.

We stood there, perplexed as to which causeway and opening we were meant to take. For all along the left hand wall, there were holes marked one to ten, while on the face straight ahead, the apertures were numbered eleven to fifteen, and then one, slightly lower and over to my right, that had the words *Other Holes* painted in white above it. And along the wall on the right, the openings were numbered sixteen to twenty. Back at the hotel, I remembered, that we had we'd been told take the hole marked 15a, however, clearly, no such aperture existed in the wall in front of us.

"I think we should go through the one marked *Other Holes*." Peter, then the most logically inclined among us, proposed cer-emoniously. "My presumption is that that hole is supposed to subsume the fictitious hole number 15a," he added rather pompously.

Since no one had a better suggestion, we all hoisted our-selves onto the causeway leading toward this opening, the one marked *Other Holes*. We skimmed along as we came closer and closer to this cavity. The slipway was extremely filthy and muddy, and it was clear from the accumulation that there had not been too many users of this pathway in the recent past. The lateness of the season was also apparent from the paucity of visitors; we were the only tourists in evidence. The facilities were not being cleaned and maintained as well as they might have been in high season, we surmised.

Marcia and Susan, who were the keenest to get to the refresh-ing water on the other side, were far in advance of Peter and me along the causeway. We two were much more leisurely in our approach. Eventually, though, first my brother, then I, too, entered from the late afternoon sun into the gloom of the cave. The passageway rapidly became narrower and darker, and the air in here was distinctly colder and clammier. Slime oozed from the floor, dripped from the ceiling, and seeped out of the walls.

As we continued our uncontrolled descent, suddenly, in the blackness up ahead, we perceived a strange mound. It seemed almost alive, very organic in its aspect, looming there in the middle of the slide. Perched on top of this rise, caressing it sensually, were two of the most horrific beasts I have ever seen. The scaly monsters moaned threateningly in our direction. Terrified, we panicked, and in unvoiced unanimity, scurried back up the passageway, defying laws of gravity, friction, and god knew what else. The brutes slowly detached themselves from the soothing comfort of their obscene mound and lumbered relentlessly after us.

Peter, who had stayed further back after our entry into the grotto, reached the opening first.

"Help! Help!" I implored him as I saw him about to clamber out of the cave through the aperture. "Peter, please don't leave me behind to the mercy of these slimy, terrible creatures."

My dear brother risked his life to offer his hand first to me and then to Marcia and Susan, who had also scrambled back up, panting and out of breath. He waited there in the entrance, holding on to the edge of the cavern with one hand and reaching back down to pull each of us up the causeway, out of the greasy cave. Hands joined, in tribal teamwork, we struggled to skate back up the slide, down which, just a short while earlier, we had coasted so easily the other way.

The slippery causeways hung over a murky swamp filled with crocodiles and other reptilian life. They led from the grotto openings to the asphalt mound, on the other side of which we hoped my parents would still be waiting for us. As I took the last few strides to reach the top of the incline, I broke off a statue of a naked woman, thinking it was an antique sculpture of a Greek goddess. Coming to a panting stop beside Peter, who had summited first, I took a closer look at my prize, only to discover to my disgust that it was the plastic skin of a mud-caked Farah Fawcett doll. I threw it into the marsh for the crocodiles to fight over.

From the top of the incline, Peter and I looked back across the swamp toward the cave-like openings that supposedly led through the rise to the swimming holes we would now never know. All of a sudden, without giving us any notice, Marcia bolted over to the Guardian of the Holes, a good-looking woman of about thirty-five, dressed in an aluminum-tinted, space-age jumpsuit, who was in the midst of talking to some other clients in front of hole number sixteen.

Marcia frantically pointed behind her, in the direction of the cave, to where one of the beasts was just sticking its head through the opening. From our vantage point, we saw the Guardian peel herself away, laughing, from the people she was talking to and make her way over to greet the monsters with a friendly smile and welcoming words. Marcia, however, was not about to take any chances; she took one look and continued her panic-stricken gallop up the slope to join us back up on the summit with Susan. As I embraced her and tried to calm her, the Guardian, leading two beautiful nymphs clad only in see-through veils, passed by us, and smiling, yelled over to Marcia.

"There really was no need to worry. These girls are just the concubines of the king, not horrific beasts at all."

"What did that woman say?" Susan, who was slightly deaf and still trembling with fear, asked my brother.

"Oh, you know . . . that those women were just the girlfriends of the king," Peter said tactfully.

"Oh, good," Susan responded, seemingly satisfied.

We didn't stay long in this shocked state of trance. Soon, Peter led us down the other side of the incline to where the van was waiting with my parents. Through the window of the cab, Peter launched into the story of our strange adventure at the swimming hole. My father woke from his slumbers and rubbed his eyes, smiling knowingly upon hearing our wild tale. My mother, who was flipping patiently through a back issue of *Time*, occasionally glanced up from it.

We piled into the van, and my father drove off into the void.

Game, in Eight Scenes

Scene I

The scene was truly bucolic. I could not help but think, as I leaned casually on the pitchfork I'd been wielding, how much it reminded me of an opera I had seen a long time ago—yes, *The Bartered Bride*, by that Czech composer, Bedrich Smetana, was it not?

The tractor chugged—ever so slowly, like a slug whose shell was much too heavy—up the steep dirt road. The cart it was straining to pull was loaded so full of hay that some bales toppled off as the tractor turned at each switchback. Marcia, my parents, my brother and sisters, and some of our dearest friends, all sporting iconic farm wear—loose, checkered shirts, jeans, baggy blouses, peasant skirts, overalls, headscarves to protect the ladies' hair, straw hats for the men—gaily cavorted around the wagon and tractor, stooping to throw fallen bundles of straw back onto the cart. The resemblance to the first scene of *The Bartered Bride* was so striking I could almost hear the opening chorus.

At several points along the twisting road, the haycart almost tumbled over the side of the incline. Toward the top of the steep slope, the tractor had difficulty negotiating the last hairpin. The motor roared and bellowed as the gigantic tires searched for traction in the muddy ruts. With one last groan, though, the machine broke through to level ground and from there, the going was easier. A little farther along the now flat road, we came to what I recognized as our destination: a pleasant clearing on the right, grass-covered, surrounded on three sides by low trees and bushes.

We nudged the tractor into this meadow, easing it along the

periphery, to the far end. The men in our small party seemed to take great satisfaction from the teamwork they mustered to rock the cart and then tip it over to unload the hay, their grunts of "Heave, ho!" mingled with peals of laughter and shouts of encouragement from the ladies. Once the wagon was empty and upright again, I grabbed its tongue and maneuvered it into the bushes. Whereupon my mother came over and admonished me, saying, "Geza, I don't think that's such a good idea."

I was astonished. "Why?"

"Well, you just shouldn't leave the cart there. Don't you know that the vegetation will consume it? It's happened before. The branches will wrap all around our wagon, and it will disappear. We'll never find it again."

Peeved at being chastised, but recognizing her superior wisdom, I reluctantly moved the trailer back out into the middle of the clearing. It was only then that I noticed that over along the edge of the meadow, back in the direction from which we had come, a number of vintage luxury cars—an old Mercedes Benz, several Jaguars, Bentleys, and Rolls Royces—were neatly arrayed in front of the shrubs. I remember thinking with glee that these would all be mine, now that I had title to the property.

What a treasure! What fun! I could hardly wait to see if any of them were operational, but since there was a lot to do, I reluctantly deferred this pleasure. I returned to the hubbub of voices on the cliff where we had dumped the hay, just as Marcia, my family and friends were deciding that just beyond the pile of hay bales and the bushes would be a perfect place to build our home.

Scene II

The house was finished. This was the first time Marcia and I set eyes upon it in all its magnificence. She clapped her hands. in happiness and I leaned over and kissed her. It was beautiful, a one-story white building with numerous rooms, strange nooks and crannies, and hallways that led hither and yon. It resembled an amoeba with appendages filled with protoplasm that spread in many directions. We wandered from room to room, marveling at all this living space that now belonged to us.

We were particularly pleased with our bedroom. Although it was not too big, nor very bright, it was comfortable and with an adjoining master bathroom. This had an old-fashioned radiator, also white, matching the little ceramic floor tiles. And against the opposite wall was a small, low, white antique bathtub on claw feet with a bright blue shower curtain.

Through the door on the other side of the lavatory was a cute little alcove, with a large easy chair and a reading light standing on a red, low-pile carpet. A big double window looked out into the back yard, and it was under this casement that I decided I would store my bicycle. Not wasting a second, I ran out to fetch it and wheeled it through our bedroom and bathroom, parking my prize neatly under the window. Life could not be any better.

Scene III

The sun was out, but still, the morning was nippy. We all—Marcia, my mother, my sisters Susan and Clara, my brother Peter and his wife Sue—sat in the grass in the clearing, which now, much to my joy, was our front yard. As we played with my nephews and nieces, from afar, those of us facing the way we had come originally to happen upon this pastoral setting could see my father eagerly strutting along the road. His hands were stuck in the pockets of his tennis shorts as he gaily whistled in time to his staccato steps. When he drew abreast of us, he chirped, "Would anyone like to come and play tennis? Aunt Sári said she would meet us at the courts."

"Why would you want to play with Sári?" my mother, who never played tennis and knew nothing about the game, interjected. "All she can do is lob the ball."

"That doesn't matter," Sue came to Aunt Sári's rescue. "My parents only lob the ball, too. As long as she can get it over the net …"

"Sure, let's go," I finally gave my delayed answer to my father's query, if only to avoid a family argument. "I'd really like to play."

"Me too," Susie piped up.

"I guess I'll come too, if you need a fourth," Peter said somewhat lackadaisically.

"Why don't we jog over?" Susie proposed. "It would be good exercise."

"I'd rather take the bicycles," my father countered.

After a heated argument, Peter and Susie decided that they would jog, while my father and I opted to take Marcia's and my bicycles. My brother and sister set off toward the courts while we went to fetch the cycles. I was glad I'd placed mine under the window in the back where it would be easy to find. For Marcia's, we had to rummage around in the garage, and eventually found it under an old canvas tarpaulin way in the back.

Scene IV

My father and I left the others in the clearing and pedaled up the road toward Hyde Park. Rounding a corner, beyond which lay a long downhill stretch that made for easy coasting, to our great surprise, in the distance we saw Susie running back toward us, rather than in the direction of the tennis courts. As we drew closer, we could tell that she had a pained, exhausted look on her perspiring face. Her grey sweatsuit was completely drenched. When we pulled alongside, my father anxiously asked, "What's the matter, dear?"

"I didn't take my hormone medicine this morning," she gasped, close to tears. "I ran out of them."

"Well, that's silly. Here, I'll give you six dollars." He pulled some bills out of his always fat wallet. "You should be able to buy some pills with this . . ." Then, remembering, he added, ". . . oh, but it's Sunday, you may run into some problems." He pulled out five more one-dollar notes, saying, "Well, now you have eleven. That should be enough to get your prescriptions, even on a Sunday."

My brakes squeaked as I stopped beside them. "No, Dad. Let's make sure Susan really has enough money." And I pulled nine crumpled dollar bills out of the pocket of my shorts. "Now, Susie, you have twenty. You must be able to get the medication with that, even on a Sunday."

With her new riches, Susie jogged off in search of a drugstore while my father and I continued our cycling journey in the other direction.

Scene V

We must have been gradually gaining altitude, for the landscape was more barren and the air seemed quite rarefied. The temperature was definitely lower, too, and here and there, patches of snow dotted the fields. With supreme effort, we topped the next rise, then the muddy dirt road wound down toward the right where there was a circular clearing covered with snow.

"That's where Marcia and I usually do our exercises." I pointed to the small meadow as my father drew level with me. "Would you like to stop and do a few sit-ups?"

"No, I don't think so." He shivered. "It's a bit too cold for me up here. Besides, there is too much snow over there, don't you agree? We would just get wet and miserable."

"Yes, I suppose you're right. Let's keep going, then."

We pedaled along the edge of the clearing, all the way to the other side where the road disappeared over the cliff.

"The easiest way to get down," I said as we approached the drop and dismounted, "is to drive really fast over the edge and let go of the handlebars, then slightly raise your arms like the wings of a moth, and gently coast down."

My father was understandably rather dubious, so he bade me to go first. I straddled the bike and pedaled over the cliff, lifting my arms and turning my head to see my father follow with a skeptical frown. The feeling was truly exhilarating. The mixture of ground and snow along the cliff face cushioned us like bread pudding. We bounced down while bits broke off all around us like loose sponge cake as we succumbed to the laws of gravity.

Fortunately, we reached the bottom intact. When we collected ourselves, we both remarked on the absence of bruises and scratches on our exposed legs and arms. Our bicycles, too, had made the descent without damage, so we remounted and started the long ride home. I remarked to myself that this way of descending the cliff face was something I definitely would want to do again.

Scene VI

It was already dark when we arrived home. Marcia's anxious embrace greeted me at the doorway. She ushered us into the living room, and we were grateful for the warmth of the fire and the calming cognac she served. My father didn't stay long; he knew Marcia and I wanted to be alone, so on the pretext that my mother must be anxiously waiting for him, he emptied his snifter and took his leave. We didn't linger, either, for the day had been long and somewhat taxing.

"I don't feel very well," Marcia said as we undressed in the bedroom.

I took another look at her as I climbed in under the duvet. She was paler than usual, but still her beautiful self.

"Maybe I should call an ambulance." I was very worried, especially as Marcia did not object, so I knew it must be serious. I climbed out of bed and dialed the emergency number. The medics with an ambulance would be on its way immediately, I was told.

I lay down beside Marcia to comfort her. We cuddled and, as always, matters developed, and we made passionate love. I was pleased that afterwards, she sighed and said, "I'm feeling a little better now."

"Should I cancel the ambulance?" I asked, hoping she really was back to normal after our lovemaking.

"No, I don't think I'm that well," my gorgeous wife answered weakly, much to my dismay.

We dozed off. After a while, I woke to a distant siren. The high-pitched wail must have been muffled by the snow, but it grew ever louder as our ears tracked its approach right to our front door. The infernal screeching finally stopped, but instead of the blessed silence we were expecting, a deafening *dingdong* sounded from the doorbell.

"Should I get it?" I asked Marcia, knowing what her answer would be.

"Yes, please. I'm still not feeling so well."

Scene VII

I climbed out of bed once again, the dutiful husband I was, and went groggily to the bathroom to fetch my yukata. I found it on top of the radiator exactly where I had heaved it earlier, crumpled up on top of the radiator, then trudged back through our bedroom and descended to the main floor of the apartment.

The bell kept ringing and ringing. Angrily, I threw the heavy door open and before I could say or do anything, in stepped a huge man—if the beast could be called that—barrel-chested, dressed in black, with an elephantine head camouflaged by an oversized World War I gasmask.

"My wife is—"

The man-monster pulled a gleaming stiletto from under his cape and drove it with all his might into my exposed chest. As I fell to the ground, I had the presence of mind to yell, "Marcia, they're here!"

I must have gone out cold or died right away, for I don't even remember the feeling of my body hitting the floor.

Scene VIII

My next memory from these turbulent times is of a group of us—I think it was my colleagues Lou Pauly, Naresh Karnick, and I—in our trench coats, sitting by a table, sipping cappuccinos, in a sidewalk café.

From out of the blue, Tony Webb, our diminutive American boss, sauntered over with his hands in his pockets and a big wad of gum circulating in his mouth, leaned over Lou and said with a wink, "Well, that was one helluva game, wasn't it, fellahs?"

The Poet and the Fencing Bag

The lecture was finally about to start. The presenter, a slim, balding man with glasses, dressed in a tan suit, jeans shirt and loosened checkered red tie, approached the projector with his slides. I must say, in this day and age, I found this all somewhat old-fashioned. The man fumbled as he put the transparencies in the tray and dropped several. Then, once he had gathered them all again in a pile, he had to squint toward the light through each one to make sure he put them back in the right order. This all took time, especially as his hands shook like my father's did from Parkinson's, and the audience fidgeted anxiously, adding ambient noise to the low, annoying hum of the projector.

The lecturer finally turned around to face the crowd, then adjusted his tie and cleared his throat with a loud croak to settle the crowd. He introduced himself as Michel Bédard from Bédard Wineries, a Bordeaux-based conglomerate that owned vineyards all over the world. Marcia and I sat near the middle over on the right hand side only twenty rows back, but Bédard's strong French accent, as well as the spectators' continued rustling, made him hard to understand.

A few minutes into the slideshow, after Bédard told us that the eponymous family company owned sixty-nine wineries around the world, including some in unlikely places such as Japan, Uruguay and Vermont, I felt Marcia's hand gently brush my elbow. "Geza, I don't feel so well," she said in a feeble voice.

And when I expressed no more sympathy than an "I'm sorry . . ." as I tried to catch Bédard's introduction of their vineyards in France, Marcia continued, "I think I'd like to go."

I finally looked over at her and saw that she was indeed looking rather pale, with a green-grey mien to match her jacket. I realized I would have to forego this wine presentation, even though it was one that I'd been anticipating for months.

"Okay, dear," I sighed. "Let's scuttle out toward the side."

Marcia stood up and disturbing her startled neighbor, who eventually overcame his annoyance and deigned to pull his knees aside, we filed past several quietly fuming wine aficionados. When we made it over to the side, I grasped her elbow to make sure so she wouldn't fall and hurt herself, but also so we wouldn't become more of a spectacle. I was painfully aware by the time we finally exited through one of the side doors that the piercing eyes of the audience were on us instead of Michel Bédard.

Out in the lobby, as I desperately weighed our options, I took Marcia over to one of the comfortable armchairs. We had already checked out of our room that morning and I had overheard the receptionist say that the hotel was overbooked for the upcoming holiday weekend. Staying another night to let Marcia rest wasn't an option. In any case, I decided that the first step was to get her to a doctor as soon as possible.

I stood in line at the concierge desk thinking they might be able to suggest a nearby hospital or doctor's office, meanwhile multitasking as I anxiously looked over at Marcia, I searched for doctors on my iPhone and fretted about having missed the lecture. Once I finally got to the front of the line—which took a good ten minutes, much to my chagrin—the attendant wrote down the name and address of a clinic nearby and assured me that someone would be able to see us there.

I asked him to get our bags from the storage room and call a car for us. He pointed me to the cab stand outside, so I tipped him a fiver. Then slinging my rucksack over one shoulder and the fencing bag over the other, I started to roll the two wheeled suitcases toward where I had left Marcia. Much to my surprise, I saw that she was gone. Frantically, I looked around and finally saw her through the large glass windows standing up the driveway, looking forlornly back at me as she tried to hail a taxi. I knew, though, from the concierge that none would stop there: cabs only picked up passengers down the hill.

I waved for Marcia, indicating for her to follow me and proceeded—balancing all the bags—to where the concierge had told me the taxis made their pickup. She seemed to have gotten the message, but still, I was extremely annoyed when we missed the first car. The next one stopped, and I opened the door for my ailing wife, then went around the back to put the bags in the trunk. That proved to be a real struggle, mainly because the fencing bag was long and such an odd shape, but I was irritated that the driver just popped the boot open and didn't bother to give me a hand. I resolved not to give him much of a tip.

As the chauffeur drove off, we started talking and he told me he'd immigrated from Poland several years earlier, and that in his spare time, he was a poet. When I told him that I wrote poetry as well, driver Lawrence invited me back to his place to show me some of his work. I was delighted, since I thought it would certainly be better than waiting in a doctor's office, so we dropped Marcia off. Just in case she needed to be picked up earlier than we planned to return, he gave her his phone number and address.

At his two-story bungalow, Lawrence insisted on taking the bags inside in case he was suddenly called away for another ride. He sat me down in the kitchen, fetched two beers from the fridge—Kirins, my favorite, since my days in Japan—and handed me a dog-eared, purple spiral notebook with *Poems* written across the cover page in bold black letters.

As I read the first verse, my concentration was interrupted by the rasping voice of a woman with what did not sound very much like a Polish accent yelling from upstairs, "Larry, is that you?"

My new friend Lawrence, or Larry, shouted back, "Yes, Viv."

That didn't sound like a Polish name, either.

"Who's that with you? Billy? Make sure you offer him something to eat," the shrill instruction floated toward us from somewhere in the ether. "Larry, you know, there's some sauerkraut in the fridge."

"Sure thing, Viv," Larry bellowed as he rolled his eyes for my benefit.

"And Larry, be on the lookout for the children. They might show up," came the next directive down the stairs from Viv. In response, I heard Larry mutter under his breath, "Oh, god, that woman . . ."

I was momentarily puzzled by the mention of children, but then got back to the little volume of verse, thinking, after the first poem, that in spite of being a brow beaten husband, Larry was an amazing bard. Honking from outside interrupted my critical thinking.

"Could that be Marcia already?" I jumped up and eagerly followed my host.

Larry opened the door as a taxi came to a sudden stop in front of the house. An old woman with white hair jacked up into a bun rolled down the rear window and peered through thick spectacles. "Is this 17 Poltergeist Street?"

Larry shouted, "Not on your life, you old goofball! You got the wrong address." He dismissed her with a raucous laugh.

He waved me to a small table and two folding chairs on the little stone patio in front of the house, "Why don't we just sit here? It's really pleasant outside."

I sat on one of the rickety chairs, worried that it might break, while Larry brought out the book of poems and two more beers. We sipped our Kirins in silence, until, just as I was reading the fourth poem, I was interrupted by another screeching of tires. Looking up from the booklet, I saw that a white van had pulled up half on the sidewalk, half off. The door on the far side slammed, and the blond driver, wearing an orange uniform with *Rodentkill* in cursive white letters on the back, appeared from behind the van.

"Hey," the exterminator greeted us without glancing in our direction.

Was he Danish, I wondered? Not that it mattered. He opened the back doors, pulled out two white nearly translucent, plastic faceless dolls, and brought them over to Larry and me.

"Here are your babies, my friend." He screwed the head of one of these dolls off and handed it to me.

"No, thanks." I recoiled in disgust. "It's not mine."

When he tried to give the doll's head to Larry, he also said, "Nope. Not my baby, either."

The van driver shrugged. "Okay, then. No skin off my back," and proceeded to heave the white doll body parts back into the van. "I'll be off, then." He slammed the doors and drove off in a huff.

During all this commotion, in the background, I vaguely heard Viv's strident voice again, anxiously asking, "Larry, what's happening down there? What are you and Bill getting up to?" When no answer came, she continued: "Did you have the sauerkraut? You know Billy always asks for that . . ."

I was pleased, though that my friend ignored her, even though I could see the buildup of annoyance in his eyes.

I went back to the patio table again and sat down to read the poetry notebook while Larry sauntered inside to replenish our Kirins. I secretly hoped he would offer me some of the sauerkraut, since it would go well with the beer. Maybe a Polish kielbasa, too. I could not help that my stomach was gurgling.

The more I delved into the taxi driver's poetry, the more I thought, *Man, this guy's really good. Better than any other living poet I've read. Right up there with T.S. Eliot, Robert Lowell, and all those greats. Why isn't he published? He should be the next poet laureate, this guy.*

I was about three-quarters of the way through the little volume when another car screeched around the corner and came to a halt right in front of where I was sitting. When I saw Marcia in the driver's seat of the white Morris Mini Minor classic convertible, I jumped up to greet her with great delight.

"Wow, dear! Where did you get the wheels? Pretty classy stuff."

"The doctor lent this car to me . . ."

But I ignored her answer, as I immediately knew we had a

huge problem on our hands: for sure, we wouldn't be able to get all the bags into this puny vehicle.

"How are we going to do this, Marcia?" I kept my voice calm, even though I felt my blood pressure skyrocket. "The fencing bag is the problem. There's simply no room for it."

"Yeah, I guess you're right. I didn't think of that."

No point in getting angry, I told myself. There had to be a solution. "Larry, could I get you to send the bag to me?"

"No way, José," He shook his head. "I ain't in the shipping business. What do you take me for, dude? UPS? FedEx?"

"Would you like to buy it then, with everything inside?"

"What the fuck for? It's of no use to me. I don't fence." He laughed loudly. "Nor does Viv. We're not the three musketeers."

"I'll give you a really good price," I tried to bargain with him, but I was getting a little annoyed with my supposed new poet amigo. I didn't like the language he was using, and maybe he wasn't as good a friend as I'd thought. I even wondered whether he'd written those wonderful poems—indeed, how could he have, if he talked like that!

As we stood around the Mini trying to figure a way out of this predicament, several teenage boys—some with fags hanging out of their mouths—gathered around. One of them, wanting to be of help, picked up the offending bag and placed it across the convertible's folded roof and said, "Why don't you just put it here, like that?"

"No, no." I pulled the bag away. "We won't be able to close the top."

"Oh, sorry." He backed off and rejoined his friends.

I had yet another idea. "Would you guys like to buy the fencing bag with all the equipment inside?" I addressed the group. "There are four epées, six extra blades, some other epée parts, three body cords, and some other junk in there. Really valuable stuff!"

The boys looked at each other. The one who seemed the oldest threw his cigarette butt on the asphalt and stepped on it.

"No, thanks. We have better uses for our money." Laughing, he added, "Plus, you idiot, we don't fence. No one here does."

"Well, do you want to try and sell the bag and everything in it for me?" I threw out my last attempt. "I'll make you a deal. You can have half the money from any sale. Just send me a check for the other half once you get rid of all the stuff."

"No, man. We're not in the business of trafficking weird equipment. And I told you, you asshole, no one around here does that stupid sport. We play hockey or do track."

I was getting very annoyed and frustrated, and also worried now that we would miss our flight. So, raising my voice, I yelled to the large crowd that had assembled, "Okay, I'm going to leave this fencing bag here on the side of the road, and you all can do whatever you want with it. We have a plane to catch. Goodbye."

We took off in the Mini, Marcia and I, driving like a fiend. I never saw my fencing bag again, nor my questionable friend Larry and Viv, his annoying wife with the piercing voice.

But I did wonder lingeringly about the sauerkraut. And the kielbasa.

* * *

Many years later, while browsing in a bookstore, I picked up a little purple book. A book of poetry, with *Poems* written across the cover in bold black letters. Underneath, in smaller cursive characters, was the name of the poet: Vivian Ellsworthy.

Inside were the wonderful poems I'd read that fateful day when I became separated forever from my fencing bag.

It was Viv then who should be the next poet laureate!

And with a name like that, I doubted that either of them had ever eaten Polish kielbasa.

Fire and Escape

I

Thunder. Yes, definitely thunder. But very far away.

Like the muted explosion of shells, during the revolution, in my youth.

Closer and closer the rumbling came as I lay there, penetrating my emerging, but still drowsy consciousness. From which direction wasn't clear.

Flashes of lightning zigzagged across the sky, potent manifestations of primordial energy. Transilluminating black eyelids, metamorphosing a somnolent mind to wakefulness.

The flares during our escape across the border, way back when I was seven.

Supine beside Marcia on a futon rolled out in front of the fireplace in the cottage poised on the slope above the water, I hesitantly opened my eyes. Smack in front of me was the big picture window and through this monitor, each time lightning lit up the world, I could see the tops of conifers. Above them, water and sky, in that order. The rain was torrential. It blurred the vista and created a background drone that the thunder punctuated now and then.

I came fully awake. My senses were humming, keen as ever, almost supernaturally so. Subliminally, they detected danger. Maybe primordial fear, rather than thunder and lightning, had woken me.

Fire. Yes, fire. That was it. Rationality kicked in. The crackling noises and the acrid odor now wafting up my nasal passages could not be mistaken. I became aware of a growing orange blob in the lower left-hand corner of the picture window television screen my eyes were staring at. The fire was expanding at breakneck speed.

Without hesitating to figure out how a fire could start and develop in such heavy rain, I threw off the sheet and jumped up, screaming, "Fire!" at the maximum capacity of my vocal chords, oblivious to the fact that only Marcia might be able to hear me. And not caring that I was stark naked, I ran out onto the front porch.

The flames were already close to the house. Omnipresent newspaper sheets blew in from among the trees below the terrace and onto the roof—I do not for the life of me know how they got there—and crackled as they caught fire. The flames soon devoured the few articles of clothing Marcia had inadvertently left hanging overnight on the clothesline.

She came out onto the terrace wrapped in a sheet. She was panicky, shocked, and visibly in despair. My beautiful wife lunged toward the nearest burning bale of paper, whipped off the rain-soaked sheet, and draped it over the burning pile. Her shapely naked body stood there, illuminated by the glow from the flames.

I vaulted over the verandah's railing to gather up the paper dancing in the path of the advancing inferno. As I dashed back with my arms full, a bolt of lightning zapped the tree from beneath which I had just a moment before collected several newspaper sheets. Thoroughly shaken, but glad to have escaped frying to a crisp, I embraced Marcia, hoping to recover in her arms.

Sudden flashes of fire from the rooftop brought a new sense of impending disaster. I scurried around to the rear of the cottage on the wraparound porch and saw that some of the paper had blown up onto the roof were burning. I climbed onto the railing and hoisted myself up on the roof, scampering along the tiles. Fortunately, these were shale rather than cedar, so didn't catch fire. I beat at the flames with my bare hands, pain notwithstanding. After putting out the seventh such clump, I surveyed the roof and, to my satisfaction, noted that no more fires were likely to start there.

II

Taking a deep breath, I looked up and let my eyes travel down the slope toward the water. Much to my surprise, a group of Thais were making their way up the steep path toward the cottage. I jumped down from the roof to greet them, not remembering until after I'd landed that I was still stark naked. As was Marcia, further along the railing.

Tant pis, as she would say in her fluent French.

"The dam has burst," the first Thai to reach the porch said in a calm voice, glancing at my member as I tried to hide it with my hands. The other men's eyes followed Marcia's luscious curves as she hurried inside. "We are evacuating everyone. We need all hands to help with the dam. You must both come with us."

As the other Thais were already clambering up onto the porch, my mind raced toward a decision. We would try to slip away quietly, not go help the Thais. No doubt, the story about the dam bursting was a ruse, and they wanted to take us into custody, I was sure. But we would escape from this godforsaken place.

"You go ahead," I told the ogling men, still trying to hide my genitals with my hands. "My wife and I will come as soon as we put some clothes on. Plus, we need to make sure everything here is as safe as can be."

The Thais gave me some rather severe looks, obviously unsure of my intentions, but when they realized I wouldn't budge until they left, they reluctantly headed back down the path.

As soon as the last one disappeared around the bend, I hurried to the bedroom where Marcia was putting on her jeans and a T-shirt. I did the same while she went into the bathroom to make herself even more beautiful. Then I looked around, wanting to collect a few items. But I dithered, opening drawers and scanning the closets to see what I should take for our escape.

Finally, I plucked a wad of money from the dresser and stuffed it in my pocket. I grabbed a Swiss army knife from a shelf in the closet, but when I couldn't open the blade, I rejected it. My passport and Marcia's, then my wallet with all my cards. As I wedged it into my back pocket, I vaguely remembered that the evening before I'd called home and my father had chided me for losing my TD Bank credit card. But at least I had my Royal Bank ones I consoled myself.

III

Just then, Aunt Clara came through the side screen door. She immediately started fussing about her fur coat. "Should I take my mink winter coat with me?" And when Marcia finally came out of the bathroom, in a loud voice, she addressed her, "What do you think?"

I found her antics rather exasperating, but my dear old aunt prattled on.

"It may be safer to leave it here. I just don't know what to do."

When neither of us paid any attention to her, she disappeared from view momentarily—not, I hoped, to find her pelt. But before I knew it, she returned with a luxurious mink coat and put it on the chair in my closet. "There. That's better. It makes me feel a lot more secure."

IV

I looked around for some books, because I knew the journey would be long and, without doubt, somewhat boring.

Robbie showed up just then to see what all the chaos was about, so I asked him, "Have you guys got any miniature books I could take along? Say, *The Thorn Birds*, by any chance? I really want to read that book."

He didn't need to answer. His face betrayed the fact that they had neither the Colleen McCullough bestseller, nor indeed any other miniature books.

I was delighted when I came upon an old gas mask case among

the junk I'd collected in a drawer over the many years. This would be perfect to carry the essentials I wanted to take for our escape.

But I still hadn't found anything to read. So I went out to the living room, where, on either side of the mantelpiece, floor-to-ceiling oak shelves were stuffed with hard cover and paperback tomes. To my great satisfaction, I found a number of small, easily transportable books, among them the pamphlet entitled *Letter on the Blind* by Diderot. I stuffed them into my gas mask case for my later enjoyment.

Back in the bathroom to pee, I remembered to pick up my toothbrush and some toothpaste, which I also managed to squeeze into the small leather case. Finally, I felt that we were ready.

V

When I went out onto the terrace, I saw that one of the Thais was just rounding the corner of the path, probably to come and tell us yet again that it was time to evacuate the zone. I grabbed Marcia's hand and we rushed out the back.

The journey was indeed long and boring. The only thing I remember, other than that I read through most of it, working through the Diderot booklet several times, was that at one point, our train passed through a town with architecture that distinctly reminded me of a beautiful little town in Austria. Maybe Hallstatt on the Hallstätter See or something similar, I couldn't be totally sure . . .

VI

The next summer, after this very eventful one with the thunder and lightning, the fire, the Thais and the escape, I was reminded of my months in the wilderness by a chance comment of the woman who was living with me.

"Come, you should take care of yourself," she flirted with me as she shaved my beard. "I, at least, have mended my Lesbian ways."

I looked at her in horror, a total stranger, with those pinkish-purple wisps of facial hair.

Distasteful, I thought. Especially since my beloved wife was no longer with us. She had perished in the escape from the fire.

About the Author

Born in Budapest, Geza Tatrallyay escaped with his family from Communist Hungary in 1956 during the Revolution, immigrating to Canada. After attending the University of Toronto Schools and serving as School Captain in his final year, he attended Harvard College, graduating in 1972 with a B.A. in Human Ecology. As a Rhodes Scholar, he obtained a B.A. / M.A. in Human Sciences from Oxford University in 1974. He completed his studies with a M.Sc. from London School of Economics and Politics in 1975. Geza worked as a host in the Ontario Pavilion at Expo 70, the world's fair in Osaka, Japan, and represented Canada in epée fencing at the Montreal Olympics in 1976. His professional experience includes stints in government, international finance, and environmental entrepreneurship.

Geza is a citizen of Canada and Hungary. As a green card holder, he divides his time between Barnard, Vermont and San Francisco. He is married to Marcia. Their daughter Alexandra lives in San Francisco with her husband David and two sons, Sebastian and Orlando. Their son Nicholas lives in Nairobi with his Hungarian wife Fanni and two daughters, Sophia and Lara. Geza is the author of five novels, four memoirs, three poetry collections, and a children's picture storybook. His poems, stories, essays and articles have been published in journals in Canada and the USA. *The Mind Spins* is his first collection of short stories.